SOUTHERN GREED - LEGEND OF THE PASS

By Captain Russell D
Walker

Copyright April 2017

Amazon eBooks / Tide Walker Press

Published June 2018

Preface by Julia A Parker

Grab your chair, dig your toes into the sand and brace yourself for this intriguing beach read.

A SW Florida setting, Murder, Romance, Kidnapping, Gold, Betrayal and above all, Justice. Proving that fate always fulfills itself regardless of who interferes. Captain Walker writes of historically documented events and suggests an alternative outcome, producing a mystery that asks the question; Is the history we've been taught the truth or is this the "real" true story?

The pursuit of gold extracts a heavy price, even more so once it's found. Discover what textbooks left untold. Ruthless Spanish explorers lay waste to the Indians of South America and war with the Florida Calusa. History states the encounters were diplomatic by nature or was it purely, Southern Greed?

Now jump 497 years ahead into today's time. Fall in Love with Beth and Curt. Solve the Riddle of the Old Fisherman to reveal the location of the lost shipment of Spanish Gold. With guns blazing, be part of the rescue. Identify the Psychopathic Killer and stop the murders.

Remember: For Those Obsessed with Greed, Justice will come.

Edition: First

ACKNOWLEDGMENT

A Very Special Thanks to my wonderful and intelligent wife Julia Ann Parker Walker for her insight and contribution to the storyline and characters. It was a joy jamming with you while sipping our wine cocktails each night in the pool building the story. We made it happen together. Thanks Florida: Everywhere I look, such inspiration for the perspiration, all the sights, sounds and tropical places.

Find the Captain in Cape Coral, Florida
Fabulous Florida Fishing
www.tidewalkercharters.com

TABLE OF CONTENTS PAGE

END

* * *

Chapter: One The Legend Begins

The year is 1518, The ship is the Neustria Senora De Madrid. A fearsome, 80-gun, Spanish Galleon, rests at anchor in the protected sound, just south of the island, between Port-de-Paix and the Ile de La Tortue, in the upper western end of the peninsula of western Hispaniola.

Her Captain, Don Cerro Estevado, is a likeable young man who was groomed for just such a position as the one he now holds. Born into a wealthy, influential Spanish family, he carries on a family tradition of men at sea. Always well-dressed, he stands 5''10" tall, of medium build with dark hair and dark eyes. Well educated in Spain and moves with an air of confidence. He has acquired a wealth of knowledge pertaining to ships, acquired at an early age, while sailing with his father. Don Cerro Estevado is also an excellent swordsman and an accomplished marksman with both pistol and rifle musket. Even with everything he had going for himself, like so many men, he wanted more.

At the early age of 25, as a show of gratitude for his bravery and loyal service to the homeland in naval battles against England, Don Cerro was given the command of a ship and a sizable land concession to govern in upper western Hispaniola by the King of Spain.

Good with family, his wife and two daughters, love him dearly. For his age, he has become quite successful as was noted by the impressive size of his ranch, which covers most of the area there on the upper eastern peninsula on the island. Unlike other Spanish landowners, Don Cerro, preferred to hire the locals in lieu of keeping slaves to work on his land. Seeking loyalty, he employed many of the locals at a fair, if not even greater than average wage, to maintain his property.

Don Cerro believed that a man working for personal gain with something to look forward too, was a happy man, loyal and one he could trust. In recent years, Don Cerro had planted at least 40% of his of land to grow sugar cane as a very profitable export. His decision to do so proved to be very wise. So much so that it rivaled profits of the silk traders in the far eastern lands. Overseeing the crop, raising of the essentials such as food and livestock, occupied most of his time. Very well-liked by all, there was not one man within his employee that certainly, would not have killed for him.

Don Cerro Estevado or "Don" better yet, "The Don", as he was known, had built a large home for himself and his wife, in which to raise their two daughters. His lovely bride, Elena, was also from Spain. She, too, was raised in an influential family. The Don and Elena were a handsome couple and are now expecting their 3rd child to be born within 4 months or less.

For being such a long way from Spain, the home was most adequate. One might compare it to an early Pre- Civil War, Southern American Plantation home in size. To be for sure though, it was of Spanish design and décor. Stately white proved to be an exterior color more prone to stay a bit cooler in the tropics, it could be seen atop the hill for many miles out to sea.

There was no lighthouse in the immediate area, so the Whitehouse was sometimes used as a landmark for navigation during dimly lit daylight hours. Knowing who lived there, some traveling Captains would refer to the coastal sighting of the house as the "Light of Don".

The home was spacious with 6 bedrooms found on the upper floor, while the master bedroom was located on the main level. On the western end of the house, a two-story Grand Room was to be found for entertaining, social and family gatherings. The homes elegance spread from an entrance living level, on upwards to the upper floor via a spacious semi-circular staircase with rooms totaling 21. This included a wash and bathing room of considerable size on the first floor. Most unusual for the times.

The geographical location of the house was founded due to the availability of a natural spring. Outside on a separate and more recently built system, spring water filled a large wooden, dark creosol sealed the outer barrel mounted on a stilted structure. Daily exposure to the tropic sun heated the water in the barrel producing the pleasure of a nice warm bath or shower upon demand, whichever the bather preferred.

For cooking and cleaning, water was continually supplied via copper piping to the kitchen by natural spring force, into a large continually draining, Talavera, ornately colored, fired sink. Very handy considering the family was still growing. With dedication, he raised his horses and livestock. A number his employees were continually busy, growing vegetables and other crops. Like many successful men though, what holdings or wealth would ever be enough?

Now, six years have passed since he had gained his commission and land concession. There, He remains governor of Western Hispaniola by royal appointment.

Outwardly and behaviorally, he appeared to be completely legitimate, after all he was the Don and Captain appointed by the King of Spain himself. How could he be anything but, "of the establishment"?

Time passes. Things change and so do people. Over the years being in in such a powerful position, he had managed to establish ties with some very unscrupulous people and some who could even be described as shady characters that sailed the Atlantic and Caribbean waters. These were men that were known as privateers, mercenaries and soldiers of fortune to be exact.

With almost perfect timing, an order from the King of Spain had arrived via Caravel messenger ship which pressed upon Don Cerro that another attempt to contact the native Indians of southern La Florida was needed. Contact that must be made if the King of Spain was going to secure a greater position in that region in the new world. From the instruction letter accompanying the decree, the King was very impatient and emphatic that the task was to be carried out as quickly as possible. Don Cerro would be required to leave his home and family to make this voyage within the next three months per the covenants of the order.

"Dearest Esposa Elena, come to me my dear. There is a matter of utmost importance that I must speak to you about. Ninas, please come to the table and join your mother and me in this conversation as this will affect you also."

"Si, Padre, what is it that is so important? Is everything alright?"

"Si, Padre, we are never told anything about your business or other matters. What could it possibly be, that we are to be included? Are we being called back to Spain?"

"Papa, will be leaving here?"

"No dearest one, we will not be leaving our beautiful home here on the island."

"As you know, yesterday, a ship arrived here from Spain, our homeland and I have just received orders, along with a decree from the King. It seems that the King has greater visions for the new world and wishes to acquire a much stronger position in the area to the northwest in La Floridas."

"I am to commence preparation immediately for a voyage that will take me away from you all for a brief period of time."

"Oh, my dearest, how long must you be gone from us. What will we do without you here? What if the baby..."

"Now calm down Elena, I promise I'll be back before the baby is born. It's only a quick trip to La Floridas."

"Si, Padre. How long will you be gone?"

"I'm thinking just over a month at the most. It shouldn't take any more than that to accomplish what the decree requires."

"But, Papa, I don't want you to go."

"Now, now little one, everything will be fine, and the time of my absence will pass quickly. You and your sister just make sure that you take care of all the chickens and the baby lamb. I'll be back before you can say Gibraltar."

"You will all be fine mi familia."

"Elena, our foreman, Senior Engoro will be nearby in my absence and provide strength and protection in the event it is needed. I have already informed him that, in my absence, it is he that you must look to for anything that I would normally provide."

"As Captain, I, along with the ship and crew, are now officially required to conduct another diplomatic or humanitarian mission for the King."

In other words, he was to make another near impossible attempt to improve relations with the hostel Florida Indian tribes in the island area of Captiva and Boca Grande, discovered in 1511 by another Spanish explorer. This mission was to be carried out quickly, hoping to keep the French and English at bay and out of the area that had come to be known as the Gulf of Mexico.

His mind raced as he contemplated the voyage. Personal gain would be his greatest motivator. It was obvious that before the trip to La Florida for the King would be carried out, Don Cerro had an agenda of his own. The timing was perfect, and his plan would be completely cloaked, as well as funded as a mission to Florida for the King. If he could pull this off, his loyalty to the King of Spain may no longer be required. But he had to be careful. Greed had been the downfall of many a good man.

Nonetheless, Don Cerro set about putting his plan into action. Immediately, he contacted an old friend, a Merchant Captain passing through port. Don Cerro commissioned and sent a messenger along with him aboard the small trade ship that was headed for Panama. There, the messenger would outline Don Cerro's plan to the mercenaries that "The Don" wished to hire.

The Don himself planned to leave within a month and a half as the Neustria Senora De Madrid needed some minor repair work that had to be done. Additionally, it had to be adequately loaded with enough provisions and supplies for the additional length of voyage. Two months and two weeks passed quickly.

"Oh, Mi Marido, please be so careful and return to me and the girls. I can't imagine living in a world without you in it. Promise me you won't take any chances with those savages in the Floridas. Promise me."

"I promise you my dear. Don't be afraid Elena, I'll be back before you even miss me. And who knows, if all goes as expected we will be wealthier than you could ever imagine."

"Yes, my Love, but I am wealthy now with the richness of your love. I need nothing else. No money or gold is worth more."

"Ok, Dear, I'll be extra careful and carry lots of extra pistols for protection."

"Girls, you do as your mother asks of you and help her all you can. You know we have another little one on the way and your mother will need all the help you can give her."

"Si, Padre, we will."

"Well, Mi Esposa Bonita, I must be on my way now."

"Sobbing, thru tears, Elena cries, Oh, Don Cerro, please be so safe and come back to me."

"I will dearest. You have my word on it. Just Calm down now. Nothing could keep me away from you my love."

"Adios Padre, Hasta mas tarde."

"Adios, mi dulce ninas."

"Hasta Pronto Mi Esposa."

"I will", he replied.

Don Cerro left the company of his family and proceeded toward the point of the ships mooring. His crew awaited upon his arrival to give the order to hoist anchor and begin the voyage.

Once underway, Don Cerro set course towards the west. Under the guise of an official Spanish mission, to the assigned area off the La Florida coast on official business for the King, Don Cerro secretly set sail and turned to the southwest towards the Port of Colon', Panama. There he was to pick up an undocumented cargo. With smooth waters and light westerly wind opposition, Don Cerro calculated that the voyage should go well without problems. That it may possibly even be completed in record time.

Upon arrival at the Port of Colon the ship and crew eased into the sleepy harbor making an unannounced docking without aid of the local Pilot. Unnoticed, throughout the night, the crew worked tirelessly to load the ship with the undisclosed cargo. The activity went virtually un-noticed. Don Cerro paid the mercenaries had hired handsomely for their effort. Promising them more upon his return when the job was fully completed on the other end. Once the last chest was brought aboard, the crew of the big ship cast off the dock lines and uncommonly, set sail into the night before dawn. She set sail back towards the La

Floridas, retracing the voyage back to the north and east, returning then, to her original mission.

After an uneventful passage, aided by the consistent westerly winds, the Neustria Senora De Madrid safely reached her second destination. The Don was back on track now to do the King's bidding.

For Three days they sailed back northeastward, along the middle and upper Matecumbes to the Peninsula of the La Floridas. Near Cuba. Turning north towards their destination.

Just as light grew dim that evening, the crew quickly lowered sail as they pulled into a point of anchorage safety. Chains clattered and clanked as the massive anchors dropped. The current was strong as usual, but the anchors held fast. Exhausted, all aboard were now to be afforded a much-needed rest.

Time passed quickly. Dawn stole the darkness from the night causing the pitch black of night to ease its grip on the lower eastern sky. The early eastern sky was askew with color as the arc of the rising sun burned brightly into an abstract of purple-gray skies contained within the lower morning haze. Excited sea birds circled noisily in anticipation of the visual freedom, soon to be granted. The sun crested on the horizon finding the Spanish Navy's, finest lady of the fleet, at anchor. The Nuestra Senora de Madrid rested, anchored into the outgoing channel current, gulf side, just off the big sandbar, outside of Boca Grande Pass.

Anchorage at this place was not strange to Spanish Captains for many times they had rested in the safety of the protected waters there. Yesterday's dusk provided rest and a well-earned end to the day for the men. The Voyage to and from Colon had extracted a great deal of energy from the crew. Sailing carefully on the return, they had navigated through the shallow Caribbean Sea and along the barrier islands of the Los Martyrs, into the Gulf of Mexico to Boca Grande pass, the mouth of Charlotte harbor, their immediate location.

Welcoming the new day, the ship's deck came alive as each member of the crew tended to his daily duties and vessel maintenance. The lamps aboard the ship deck posts were filled with oil in anticipation of the later evening's activities. A celebration of success would be held by order of the Captain which, included consuming the large barrel of rum stored in the ship's hull.

But, for now, this morning, the small launch crafts were boarded and lowered. Each boat headed towards the mainland yet on separate courses. Splitting up, so to speak, to find a source of fresh drinking water. Water needed to replenish and re-fill the barrels stored on board the ship.

And so, they did explore the area for what it would yield from water to fruit. Sometimes a wild boar would also be taken but, not so on this day. The waters here seemed so alive. Early May always yielded a spectacular sight in the waters of Boca Grande where thousands of Tarpon would roll at the surface with the changing tides. Fish the Spanish considered worthless. They were beautiful but no good, whatsoever, to eat.

Under cover of hay and straw, deep within the ship's hull, lay chests of gold, silver bars and thousands of coins stored in small trunks. Many other artifacts of treasure were also stored and lashed to the ship's inner spars and hull. Treasure that had been plundered. Savagely, taken by order of the ship's own Captain by his hired band of inland mercenaries and privateer soldiers from the Indians in the Upper Eastern range of Columbia, South America. When completed, the success of this venture would be highly profitable for all involved.

Though the Captain sailed under the flag of the King of Spain, Don Cerro Estevado himself was a privateer at heart. It was his full intention to short the King monetarily and cash in on his recently acquired cargo to pre-arranged buyers that awaited him in Port Royal. After all, the King was a long way away.

The ship's crew would also share a portion of the take which caused a much-needed lift in the moral, lifting the spirits of the men who had all worked so hard. Returning to the tasks at hand. Cheerfully, the crew had fully restored the ships' water supply and made some minor repairs. There would be celebration tonight, for tomorrow; they would attempt the much-dreaded meeting with the Calusa Indians of Useppa and the village of Tampa area on northern Pineland Island.

The Calusa Indians had occupied the region from 100 BC, for nearly 1700 years. The men were tall and well-built with long black hair. Calusa means "fierce people," and they were described as a fierce and war-like. With the first meeting, the Spanish explorers found that these Indians were fierce and unfriendly. The explorers soon became the targets of the Calusa attacks.

The Calusa had many weapons and developed a warlike weapon called an AtlAtl. This weapon, in the hands of an accomplished warrior, could launch a 6' long light obsidian tipped spear with great accuracy at almost twice the distance that one could be thrown by hand alone. Many local tribes paid homage to the Calusa for protection. Including the Miami, Seminole and the Miccosukee Tribes.

This Indian tribe was the first one that the Spanish explorers wrote home about in 1513. The Calusa wished to have no contact with the Spanish. They believed the Spanish wanted only to destroy them and take their lands. In addition, diseases such as smallpox and measles were brought into the area from the Spanish explorers and these diseases wiped out entire villages. The Calusa came to hate the Spanish and all other white men as a result including, the French and English. Calusa Chief was known as Chief Caalus which the Spanish quickly changed reference to him as Chief Carlos.

The Calusa Indians did not farm like the other Indian tribes in Florida. Instead, they fished for food on the coast, bays and rivers. The Calusa lived along the inner waterways near the coast. Most families built their homes on stilts. The people, men and boys of the tribe made nets from palm and Palmetto tree webbing to catch mullet, snapper, jacks and other table fare granted by the sea. They used spears with long jagged points to acquire eels and spear sea turtles. They made arrowheads from fishbone, used when hunting for animals such as deer and hog as they were plentiful on the islands. The women and children learned to catch shellfish like conchs, crabs, clams, lobsters, and oysters. They were sometimes known as the Shell Indians or Fish People.

Many times, the Spanish had attempted to repair relations with the Calusa tribe but to no avail. This attempted meeting was by order of the King of Spain himself, so an attempt had to be made regardless of the outcome. But, tonight, for the crew and all on board, there would be a celebration.

As dusk fell once again upon the area, lamps were lit on deck. Music of the fiddle, harmonica, spoon board and a makeshift drum permeated the air and everyone's senses, while the crew made merry in celebration. The smell of tobacco being smoked occasionally scented the air. Laughter and singing could be heard from afar. Some men danced merrily around the main mast base while sporting their mugs of rum. Their newfound wealth seemed even greater to them as the influences of the rum lifted their spirits. Unaware that the evening could produce anything but pleasure. Consumed in celebration, the crew and officers on board were oblivious to anything happening outside the ship's railing.

Now, under complete cover of darkness, the Calusa Indian warriors paddled towards the ship preparing to attack the unsuspecting men aboard the Spanish Galleon, Neustria Senora De Madrid, which was resting peacefully at anchor. Not a single sole on board the ship sensed what was about to happen.

With incredible stealth, thru the darkness, at slack tide, 35 Blackened Calusa War Canoes arrived alongside the stately ship. With the aid of insulated clay pots, on the floors of the canoes, which held red hot coals that provided the source needed to lite the long and deadly flaming arrows. In unison, they're long arrows were lit and launched at the ship. Initially, The Calusa warriors sent three volleys of flaming arrows into her mast, rigging and hull. The ship was thoroughly set ablaze as the unarmed and confused conquistadors, soldiers and sailors onboard the ship rose to make opposition.

The Calusa warriors were ready for them, targeting each man on board with deadly accuracy. Volley after volley, the warriors launched their obsidian tipped, wooden arrows of death and destruction. Each one treated with the poisonous sap from the native Manchineel apple tree. With no immediate weapons at the crew's disposal, all the men aboard were sitting ducks. Most of the crewmen were struck repeatedly by the continued volleys of the Calusa arrows. Blood poured from the wounds of the stricken men virtually covering the ships flooring, making the wooden ship's deck slick and all but impossible to move about on, much less escape. Over and over volleys of arrows stuck down even unto the last of the remaining man.

Cries from the men outside stirred the captain from the safety of his cabin. Don Cerro emerged only to be struck instantly by two Calusa war arrows. One arrow struck sideways, through his chest and one frontal hit through his neck. Gasping, falling to his knees, he grabbed at the arrow in his chest, continuing to fall down onto his face where the angling arrow in his neck hit the deck causing his head to turn sharply. The snap of his neck could be heard even unto the canoes below. Then, only the sound of the ever-crackling breathing of the flames consuming the ships timbers could be heard. Don Cerro Estevado would not enjoy the fantastic wealth he sought. What's more, he would never return to his home or his family as originally planned. Nor, would he ever see the newborn baby his wife was about to bring into the world. The Greed that had consumed him had also cost him his life.

It's amazing how many times the pursuit of wealth, even with the best laid plans, ultimately, can cost a man his life.

That night was now etched into Clausa history.

With no movement to be seen aboard the ship the vicious Calusa attack ceased. The timbers of the good ship continued to burn throughout the night, right down to the waterline, sinking there at anchor. Not a single man onboard the ship survived the vicious onslaught of the Calusa attack.

* * *

Chapter Two: Lightning Strikes Twice.

The Calusa Indians made a practice of raiding ships sunk close to their shores. They found it beneficial to recover ropes, nails, iron rods, tools and even some food stuffs. They were not unfamiliar with the Spanish, their tactics, there gifts, their lies and the disease they sometimes brought with them. In the years gone by starting in 1510, the Calusa learned about the benefits and the detriments of dealing with the Spanish Race. They soon grew to hate the Spanish for their cruelty and what they did to the Calusa people. The Calusa warred against them at every opportunity afforded them.

Upon salvaging this particular ship, the Calusa discovered the treasure hidden deep in her hull. Calusa men were able to dive to great depths upon a single breath which aided them greatly in the recovery. The remaining, unburned portion of the ship now lay in 30 feet of water. Through toil and heavy labor, most of the gold bars and trunks of coins were recovered thru the Calusa's effort. However, late in the process, a severe storm blew into the localized area and destroyed what was left of the great ship. Breaking from anchor, the hull and timbers were mostly disintegrated by the high winds and extreme pounding in the shallow surf. The two remaining trunks filled with gold coins were both loosed from their storage and dashed against the hard bottom, strewn across the sand even to the point of rocks at the mouth of the pass.

Though the gold was of no real value to the Calusa, they knew only too well that the Spanish would kill to obtain it and that people of other lands found gold and silver very valuable and prized it greatly. With this knowledge, the great Calusa Chief, Caluus, gave the order that a containment vault would be made from a nearby, partially submerged Limestone outcrop where all the treasure would be placed.

A small karst remnant of an ancient limestone reef which had been uplifted then eroded due to occasional exposure to fresh water. I.E.; a small key cave nearby, partially underwater near Pine Island between the islands of Useppa and Cayo Costa, which could be used to forever hide the cargo, so dangerous to the safety of the people of the Calusa Village there on Pine Island.

It was therefore forbidden by the Calusa Indian King and decreed that it was punishable by death for anyone to speak of or divulge where the treasure could be found. No words were ever muttered by the Calusa for fear of receiving the wrath of the decree.

Once the tiny island had been loaded with the forbidden cargo. The entrance was sealed with many layers of heavy conch shells, packed and covered in a roman-like, limestone mortar known to be used by the Calusa in those days.

The loosened coins sparsely littered the sub-surface sands of the pass area for hundreds of years. They were rarely but, occasionally found. These coins being the only remnants left of the cargo carried by the Senora Nuestra de Madrid on that fateful day the Calusa warriors attacked her.

The coins being the only evidence left to create a Legend that would be talked about for many hundreds of years to come.

With the passing of Don Cerro and the disappearance of the Nuestra Senora De Madrid, the Kings agenda to befriend the Indians of La Florida was fatefully postponed. A situation that the King was most unhappy about. Other Captains were subsequently commissioned to make attempts to accomplish the same goal. The King wished so much for this feat to be completed that he offered up the Governorship of Puerto Rico to whomever proved to be successful in accomplishing the task. A Governorship that already belonged to the Spanish explorer, Juan Ponce de Leon.

Now in Spain, while preparing for the voyage back to Puerto Rico, Juan Ponce de Leon learned that there had recently been at least two unauthorized voyages to "his" Florida discovery both ending in repulsion by the Native Calusa Tequesta warriors. Ponce de León realized he had to act soon if he was to maintain his claim on the Governorship.

Once again, to retain his commission in Puerto Rico, and traveling under the Spanish flag of Humanitarianism, Juan Ponce de Leon, in his own ship arrived at the site where the Don Cerro's vessel had supposedly sunk. Though the trip was, once again, officially listed as a government relations improvement journey, the underlying reason for this return voyage by Ponce de Leon to those exact lands that he himself had discovered, was to find and recover the treasure. From the information, he had received from his friends in the Central Americas, Panama area, Ponce de Leon thought for sure that the treasure existed, and that the legend was indeed true. He had returned to the exact spot the ship was supposed to have been to separate fact from Legend once and for all.

On July 1521, upon arriving at the mouth of Boca Grande Pass, Juan Ponce de Leon and his crew dropped the anchors of his good ship the Santiago. It had been a very long journey from Spain with only a short stop in Cuba, affording only enough time for supplies and water to be taken aboard. The crew needed rest. Juan Ponce de Leon seemed nervous, scattered and otherwise irritable. It appears that he was focused on things other than those immediately at hand. Perhaps thoughts of treasure, gold, silver. Maybe the last moments Neustria Senora de Madrid occupied his mind. Having dealt with the Calusa previously, Juan Ponce de Leon knew that the Calusa could show up at any time without warning, which only added to the anxiety. With an enemy that fierce at hand, it would tend to make even the most seasoned Captain a bit nervous.

As the tiny lights of fireflies began to make themselves evident over the water in the immediate area around the ship, the sun set to the west. Given life by the oncoming sea breeze, the palm fronds moved in unison, bowing, turning and twisting as if to celebrate the chance to dance with one another again.

Gulf waves produced crisp sounds as they continually moved against the shoreline. The monotonous, repetitiveness of the sound became almost trancelike. Night was upon them. With the sails drawn in tight to the mast and yardarms, an uneventful slapping of the rigging could be heard along with an occasional scream of a passing gull looking for roost.

The Santiago was a ship of great stature. Three masts sported much canvas to catch the exhaled breath of the great westerlies for propulsion. With three decks above the water line, two, of which, were both lined, each side with 25 canon doors made it an equal, if not greater than any other adversary in most occasions of disagreement. But for now, she rested quietly in the turquoise clear waters of La Florida at the mouth of pass known as Boca Grande.

Darkness was opposed by many whale oil lamps lit in strategic positions and set about the upper deck of the ship. The men made their way about and gathered around the stew cistern. Eating, resting, laughing and telling stories of other voyages.

Though the men of the Santiago were at ease for the evening meal, they remained alert, cognoscente of Calusa war tactics, the men knew the Calusa were capable of unannounced attacks. With that knowledge, the men had placed guns and weapons in various places about the deck, just in case they were needed.

Surprise is always the best weapon when outmanned and up against superior numbers. An unannounced, unprovoked, attack, had always worked well for the Calusa warriors.

Ending this day, darkness cloaked the Calusa warrior's arrival at the side of the Galleon. Without so much as a splash to announce the onslaught, Volley after volley, the warriors launched their poison tipped arrows up and over the ships rails at the men on deck of the Santiago.

Instantly, the men jumped into action, grabbing up the nearby pistols and their single shot rifles. Over the rail, they returned as much fire as possible. In the pitch black of night, it was like shooting a target that could not be seen. Rarely if any of the ghostlike Calusa foes below in their blackened war canoes were hit. This night's battle would prove to be no exception. With precision though, the Calusa Warrior's onslaught sent volleys of long flaming arrows into the ships mast, rigging and hull.

Almost identical to the experience of Don Cerro Estevado years before, Juan Ponce de Leon was alone in his cabin finishing his evening meal when he heard the nose of the fight. Quickly, he emerged from his position, aft ship. A Calusa arrow rocketed thru the air, narrowly missing him, striking deep into the wood of the now open door of his cabin, with a loud crushing "Thunk". Another flaming arrow, singed his hair, finding it's mark in the cabin wall, barely missing his forehead. The stench of his own burning hair choked him. Avoiding other projectiles, he dove behind the mast base next to the aft wooden water barrel. He grabbed the handle of the large, round wooden barrel lid holding it in front of himself for protection.

With two pistols, one in his belt and the other in hand he held the makeshift shield to protect his upper torso and backed up quickly behind the main sail mast. There, he then gathered his courage, lifted the shield and began to make his way to the ships railing to return fire. Two short war arrows instantly ripped into the wooden barrier. He held it closely to protect his head and chest.

Hissing like a striking viper through the air, with a horrible thud, a Calusa war arrow viciously struck under the protective shield into his upper right thigh. The shattered the femur bone exhibited the bloody arrow point sticking out his leg. Crying out in agonizing pain, Ponce de Leon struggled to make it back to the safety of the huge iron like center mast. With all his might he cried out for the men on the upper first deck to return a volley of cannon fire at the warriors and to hoist the anchors. A row of canon fire belched forth fire and lead into the pitch black of night. No enemy was hit. Nothing save a large spray of water as a finale to the cannonballs flight. Only the explosive noise

23

was threatening for no canoe or Indian was hit with any of the launched projectiles.

The now increasing outgoing current caught the great ship as the anchors freed themselves from the sandy bottom of the pass. Slowly they drifted away from the immediate vicinity of the attack. Juan Ponce de Leon had succumbed to the pain of the wound where he lay slumped over near midship, where his men found him later, unconscious, still clutching the water barrel lid for protection. The men picked him up and took him back to his cabin. Then, returning to the deck to put out the remaining fires onboard the ship.

Morning came. The remainder of the crew, nursed their wounds, gathered their composure, and slowly set the sails towards the Port of Havana in Cuba. Upon reaching port, two days later, Juan Ponce de Leon died. He had succumbed to infection of the terrible wound inflicted by the poisoned arrow used by the Calusa. Lightning had indeed stuck twice, and the incident will be forever remembered as the Battle of Boca Grande Pass. Wealth was the incentive, but Greed had claimed yet another life.

Now, more than 497 years have passed.

The Calusa Indians are now long gone. Ruling and inhabiting the area, they were there from 100 B.C. on, until the 1570's. Later years saw the mighty Calusa driven out by slavers into the Everglades. Diffused into the Miami, Miccosukee and Seminole tribes. Today, no true Calusa Indian remains alive. No true Calusa blood line exists from those days. Nothing but an occasional crude gold coin is to be found on the beach to substantiate the mystery and the origin of the legendary treasure of Boca Grande Pass.

Chapter Three: A Chance Meeting

Elizabeth Blaire Higgins. Beth, as she is most commonly called by her friends. A true Florida Cracker, dark haired and intelligent. Her passion for the secrets of the earth's buried historical treasures is outweighed only by her zest for life.

She's tall, standing just under 5' 10". Her frame disperses her strengths into long, smooth symphonic lines of beauty. She is graceful in movement. Her breasts are of average size, yet a compliment to her overall feminine look. Desirable is a good word. She is confident. Her hair, long and black, usually worn up, sort of, in a hive like affair, caresses a rounded forehead and spills its color in the direction of her natural olive skin. A conservative yet pronounced nose sets the foundation for her striking and unusual look. Blessed with large medium green eyes, lightning could only be compared to the flash they reveal when she was in competitive thought. Yet, when at rest, these emerald mirrors subtly radiate the life that lives within, changing color only slightly with her mood. Her medium sized lips are complimented on either side by slightly mischievous dimples, content to reveal themselves only when she smiles.

With her sunglasses shoved into her hair above her forehead, today she is dressed as she typically does. A colorful flower print Florida Camp shirt adorns her upper torso complete with medium collar and shirt pocket. Almost nerd like, she always carries a ballpoint pen in the pocket claiming she is in constant need of it. Her shorts are mid length with two tassels on the outer side of either leg, indicating a drawstring within. Her shoes are flat, thin, leather strapped, sandals with an open toe.

For a woman of her height, she does not have unusually large feet.

Early on, Beth took a Post Grad position with Florida Southwestern State College, Fort Myers as a summertime job to instruct the under graduates. In doing so, she hoped to acquire extra credit towards her Master's degree.

Time has passed since that summer. Now as chief Director of Archeology for FSW, she has headed up several digs near Lake Okeechobee, Florida which have answered many questions and have yielded many artifacts known to belong to one of the 1500-year-old main branches of the Calusa Indian Tribe and others.

Now, with her Doctorate hand, she is 31 years old. The required scholastic achievement curriculum and her dedication to uncovering historical data from multiple digs has kept her very busy. To date, marriage has never been a consideration. She remains single, dedicated to the work she loves so much.

Just two blocks west of the FSW campus is her favorite morning coffee stop. One of the busiest Starbucks you will ever find, due to its proximity to the University. Beth makes her way thru the ordering line to get her favorite coffee each morning. A Vanilla Latte, double espresso with one squirt of vanilla, low cal. Sometimes, you can hear her chant her favorite saying as she passes through the line: "Gim-me Just a little bit of Coffee, to start the day out right, help me wake those sleepy eyes up, after a long and restful night. "

After paying for her drink, she looks up to see an old friend at a table near the shop entrance. Beth makes a waving gesture towards her friend and smiles generously. Though partially blocked, her friend makes an equal effort towards Beth and waves back.

An exceptionally funny situation arises as a result. Right next to and just a bit in front of her, old time, girlfriend, coming in through the entrance door, is an exceptional figure of a man, who takes Beth's wave to be a gesture towards him.

Smiling, he makes his way towards her. "Excuse me, were you waving at me? I don't think we've met. My name is Curt. Curt Lafferty."

Major Curt Lafferty, US Marine Corp, Special Ops, AH 64E Apache Attack Helicopter pilot retired, 38 years old. At 6' tall, he is muscular and is blessed with a slightly chiseled facial look. His leathery, sun tanned skin, only adds to his appearance. The corners of his eyes are accented by crevassed, lighter lines of laughter as he is usually optimistic and cheerful. He has a full head of medium brown hair and combs it back. He sometimes finds it falling partially forward on the sides, gently cupping over his eyes, on either side of his oval shaped face.

In turn, a medium 5 O'clock shadow growth of a beard accentuates his strong, pronounced jaw line. Obviously, judging by the color of his face, he is not concerned about the dangers of too much unprotected skin sun exposure. But he's still a young man and obviously doesn't think much about it yet. His forearms exhibit strength, like that of a weightlifter or sports buff. His medium length fingers sport only partially manicured short nails. He wears no rings. His wide palms indicate the possibility of an exceptional grip. As strange as it sounds, the thick, sun lightened growth of hair on his outer forearms makes him appear invitingly cuddly. Though he walks with a slight

28

limp and utilizes the aid of a cane, he is non-the less, very attractive.

As he approached her, when eye contact was made, they both, as if in self-defense, instantly glanced to the floor. Then gradually, lifting their gaze, their eyes to meet once again. Then, with somewhat of a rush, an inspired feeling comes over both of them.

"Have we met before? Curt said.

"No, why no. Now trying to show strength, I don't think so. I'm Beth Higgins" She extends her right hand out offering a formal greeting and handshake.

"My pleasure Mam! He says with a slight touch of a southern drawl. Can I get you a coffee?" "Oh, Ha!" "I see you've already got one. Do you have time to talk for a moment?" "Surely we have time for a quick chat over the morning cup." "Interested?"

"Well, I'm pretty much in a ...,"

Looking up and back at Curt standing there, she smiles; "Why, Sure, I'll take the time." she responded. "Come. We can sit over here."

Before sitting, Curt laid the book he carried with him down on the table.

Instantly, Beth came alive. "Oh my God! The Dreamweaver. I love that book! What a remarkable story, I love it! Mel Fisher and his quest for the Spanish Galleon, the Atocha. She triumphantly declares."

"Yes, I love it too," Curt said, I'm almost halfway through it. I guess you could say I'm part history buff and part treasure hunter."

Beth suddenly looked away.

29

"I'm sorry, Curt said, did I say something wrong?"

"No. No not really. It's just that the word treasure is not a well-received word in my line of work."

"Your line of work?" he asked.

"Yes. I am the Departmental Director of Archeology, for FSW here in Fort Myers," she said proudly.

"I do love it so! Here I come all the way to Florida and what do I stumble into, nothing less than a beautiful scholastic female rock-hound. Unbelievable," Curt exclaimed excitedly. "But I'm not a treasure hunter. Ever since I was a boy back in Oklahoma. I used to explore the nearby limestone caves and look thru areas known to be near ancient Indian encampments. I looked for arrowheads or whatever I could find. It was my favorite pastime. I still have some of the arrowheads if found made by the ancient Cheyenne and Arapahoe tribes."

"Amazing, she said. As a child, I think I must have been afflicted with the same geological and historical curiosities that you were."

Talk quickly turned into curiosity for Beth. Questioning; "Who was this interesting man? What he is and how did he happened to end up at her favorite coffee shop this morning?"

For the record, there was something about this meeting. Two strangers coming together by complete accident. Two people that never knew each other whatsoever, prior to only a few minutes ago, yet they seem so completely comfortable to be so near each other now. Very Refreshing.

"Curt, do you mind telling me a little bit about yourself?"

"Why, no, I'd be happy too. Lifting his cane, smiling sheepishly, he began; I'm no one of importance, I guess, except to my mother," gently tapping his carved, Bois-d-Arc, brass tipped cane on the floor. "My name is Jonathan Curtis Lafferty. I was

30

named after my dad's best friend, a Swedish American named Jon. Dad knew him as a kid. They grew up together. He was killed in the war when he and Dad served. Curtis comes from my mother's side. Mother claimed to have many relatives sporting that name and she said it added a nice ring to Jonathan. So, they opted for that more official title instead of the name Curt, that I go by. I'm the youngest of four children. I have three brothers back in Oklahoma."

"I'm a retired Major from the U.S. Marine Corp, Special Ops, AH 64E Apache Attack Helicopter division. I'm 38 years old. I use this cane because of a broken leg I suffered in a helicopter crash during Desert Shield. That was the second Iraq conflict. I survived with some help from my buddies and I am Thankful to be alive and still here on the planet. I'm getting stronger as the years go by, but I still need this old cane, occasionally, to steady myself. I try to work out every now and then for strength and therapy. The Eagle head carved in the handle was done by a talented friend of mine back home."

"Back Home?" Beth looked questioningly.

"Well, yes, I'm from a small town in south central Oklahoma named Davis. Born and raised there. My Mother, Helen Maurie Lafferty, still lives there in a house that my Dad built there after the second world war was over."

"Dad passed away in a plane crash when I was 15 years old. Delbert Eugene Lafferty was his name, a retired WWII pilot. He had his pilot's license before he even got his driver's license. Though Dad retired from the service after the war, he still loved flying. He spent much of his time testing contemporary designs of crop duster planes that were built there locally in our hometown."

"The Davis Crop Duster Plane Corporation built planes with a monstrous radial 16-cylinder motor and new Corsair type low swept wings, the Davis Duster Planes were known for their exceptional power and excellent handling characteristics. One design, however, had extreme control surface issues or in fact an extreme flaw which, ultimately cost Dad his life. It was horrible thing for Mom, me and my brothers to get through."

"The crash was not his fault. Dad was a great pilot. I looked up to him vowing to someday become a pilot just like him. I did just that after graduating college from Oklahoma State University. I joined the Marines. I had a degree in aviation engineering and fairly good grades. That all helped me make it into to Special Forces. I opted for Helicopters instead of the fixed wing models that my dad flew."

"After returning from overseas and healing up a bit, I moved to Florida because I hated the constant threat of the Oklahoma tornadoes in the spring and fall and the dam cold winters, snow and ice. I mean, it's not like weather up around the great lakes, but it was enough to motivate me to move down here, to a more tropical and enjoyable climate. When I first started coming to Florida, I spent allot of time on the east coast in Miami. However, after a friend's invitation, I found Florida's west coast and fell in love with it. I've been here three years now. I have a little house that I bought on a canal that connects to the Caloosahatchee river across the bridge in Cape Coral and I have a little dog. His facial markings make him look like he's wearing mask. Bandit seemed like the perfect name."

"Really, she said. What kind is he?"

Laughing out loud at the thought of his dog. He looked up at the ceiling as if he could see Bandit through his mind's eye.

"He's a rescue. Part Blue Healer and part Australian Shepard. He's slim and strong. He has a beautiful multi-colored coat. Kind of Calico Black and white if you will. He's agile and fast, exceptionally smart too, as you might expect from a mutt of his caliber and he's very protective."

"Awesome", she said, "perhaps someday I'll get to meet him."
Looking at his hands, Beth noticed he wore no rings. Out of
nowhere Beth suddenly blurted out; "So... You're not married?
Oh, I'm sorry, that's really none of my business, forgive me for
being so forward."

"Oh, that's OK, think nothing of it."

There seemed to be an instant attraction between the these two,
who had met here at Starbucks, so innocently this morning.
Sometimes fate intervenes at the oddest of times or even place.

Beth subsequently told Curt a little bit about herself, her family
and her position with the University. The morning minutes were
swept by like so many gulls leaving for the coast. "Oh, My God,
It's five minutes till twelve o'clock." Beth exclaimed. "I can't
believe I've missed the entire mornings work at the office."

"I'm so sorry," Curt said. "I've kept you entirely too long. The
time just flew by."

Beth stood up and smiled at Curt. "It's not your fault. She
extended her hand and said. Think nothing of it. I've enjoyed it
and quite frankly I'm amazed that the morning has slipped by so
effortlessly. It's truly been my pleasure."

"Likewise. I believe you to be the most delightful surprise this
town has given me to date. What an incredible morning."

Smiling, Curt stands to accept her hand. Again, with that ever so
slightly southern drawl; Curt says," I certainly hope we can get
together again before too long. It is wonderful meeting you and
it's been a fun morning."

Without hesitation, Beth says; "I think that can be arranged.
Yes, I think I would like that. Here is my University card. You
can reach me at the office during..., well, here, I know I
shouldn't, barely knowing you and all but, let me give you my
cell phone number."

Beth wrote the number on the card and handed it to Curt. She was enamored by the fact that he was interested in some of the things that she was and somehow, she felt some sort of immediate attraction to Curt.

They shook hands and kinda did a quick little "Man Hug" thing. As though in a daze, Curt turned and walked out the door opposite of where he had parked his car.

Beth stood near the coffee shop door and watched Curt make his way.

Realizing he was headed in the wrong direction, he quickly turned and headed back the other way past the sidewalk. Glancing back at Beth, he smiled sheepishly and shrugged his shoulders with a kind of WTF look on his face, then continued on towards his ride.

Beth returned the smile. She remained fixated on him as he reached his car. A new, Gun Metal Gray Wrangler Rubicon, Dino Jeep, lifted with custom wheels and many extras making it appear much larger than it really was.

Just as I might have expected, Beth thought to herself. "The Ride made almost as much of a statement as the man did."

As Curt backed out of his parking place, Beth recalled the smell that hit her when he pulled her close to him. A light and pleasant smell. It wasn't after shave or cologne. Actually, it was friendly and refreshing. It Reminded her somehow of the aloe gel her mother used to put on her sunburn as a child. Perhaps it was hair gel or something. Whatever it was, she couldn't quite put her finger on it but, it seemed so pleasant, tending to make him even that much more approachable.

As Curt drove off, Beth took in a deep breath, then let out a big sigh. Involuntarily, a big smile came over her as she gathered her things to leave. Her mind raced over the possibilities.

Recalling all the conversation that morning, Curt and Beth had eventually got around to and talked a little bit about the legend of the Spanish ship, the Neustria Senora De Madrid.

A local legend handed down over the years known to many south Floridians about a sunken Spanish Galleon, of gold and of death at the hands of the Calusa Indians.

Earlier, Beth made it known to Curt that she had received a mysterious phone call the previous day, inquiring as to whether she had any information regarding it. Asking her if she thought the legend was true.

Subconsciously, Beth wondered if the chance meeting with Curt part of the scheme was somehow, possibly to find out if the treasure was real and too, perhaps, recover it. Curt's demeanor seemed very sincere though, she decided to shelve those thoughts for now.

Chapter Four: Looks are Deceiving.

American Antique Incorporated is located in Miami, Florida. Owned and operated by Agustin Matias Ribeiro, a 72-year-old antique art dealer from Brazil. He deals mostly in expensive estate pieces and otherwise special artifacts produced by the masters. Nothing contemporary is ever found in either of his two Miami stores.

Agustin always says, "It's Just not right, selling something that is not at least 200 years old."

The family also deals in very expensive estate furniture and jewelry. Occasionally, in certain archeological artifacts. Agustin married Juliana Betesma in 1948. Elegant and fashionable, a lady in her mid-60's. With the degree in accounting and management, she acquired years earlier, she oversees the family's money, investments and overall financial wellbeing. Together, they have three sons, the two oldest were born and educated at the University of Brazil.

They have both moved on to take wives and make families in America. Bernado, the oldest lives in Jacksonville Florida. He sells Yachts and has a sizable interest in a trendy hotel there.

The middle or second son, Rafael, owns a Real Estate company in Miami. Money abounds in the Miami area with such a great influx of tourists and retiring successful people, both local and from foreign lands. Miami is a real estate Mecca. Real Estate is at a premium there too, hence the many high-rise hotels to be found along the eastern emerald coast of southern Florida on down to South Beach. When real estate is at a premium, best to build straight up. Rafael and his wife do very well, enjoying tremendous annual sales of Biscayne gulf view and east coast local properties. They are also regulars at the Fountain Bleu Hilton Hotel bar scene for late afternoon cocktails.

The third and youngest son, Enrique Luis Ribeiro, was born in Miami, Florida. Perhaps he was a tad bit spoiled. He attended upper end, private schools there, where he ultimately graduated from High school. Subsequently, he enrolled at the University of Miami. Midterm of his first year of attendance, he dropped out of college due to a major controversy. Enrique or Rico as he was known, was somehow implicated in the disappearance of a very expensive Roman Catholic Christian relic held in the school chapel of the campus. Irreplaceable and considered priceless, it was never found. Due to lack of evidence, Rico was never officially charged but suspicion was high. He was subsequently asked to cease his studies at the University.

A very handsome young man at thirty-six years of age. Rico has dark hair and is medium dark skinned. He is muscular with an Adonis like build. It's hard to ignore him as he continually wears an absolutely infectious smile. Usually dressed in white or bone colored linen slacks, shorts when permitting, a blousy linen, collared shirt without pockets, the top two buttons always open.

Though he has never admitted to being very religious, he wears a chain of gold which is centered with a medium sized polished Gold St. Christopher medal suspended from it. His shoes are Italian made of polished strap leather, normally worn without sox. His cash and credit cards are hid inside a solid silver, clamp over, money clip.

Rico continues to live in Miami where he owns a travel agency. Like his father, he has combined a small retail shop that dealing in European art, furniture and estate jewelry. Located just off the Julia Tuttle Causeway, where the view of Biscayne Bay is magnificent, then up north on Alton Road, you will find Viajes Europa, his agency.

Under Rico's travel direction, trips are arranged to Europe, mainly Spain, Egypt, Portugal and France. Individuals interested in expensive art and European estate jewelry utilize his services. Ancient artifacts sometimes show up at his direction. Some are brought in from Egypt. On occasion, the agency has been suspected by authorities, as a front for trade of illegal artifacts, while he maintains that he is a legitimate business dealer of art and jewelry, just like his father. More than once though, he has been investigated for trafficking in stolen, illegal or smuggled ancient artifacts. However, to date there has never been enough evidence to arrest him.

A 2010 599 GTB Fiorano F1 Grigio Silverstone Ferrari w/ Rosso Leather Interior, with only 5 thousand miles on the odometer. A dealer Installed HGTE Package, Carbon Fiber Driving Zone, Carbon Fiber Sport Seats, complete with the full Daytona package set on the showroom floor in front of him. Red in color just as he had always dreamed his Ferrari would be.

"I'll take it!" Rico blared out, so all in the dealership showroom would hear him.

"But Sir, you haven't driven the car yet. Would you..."

"I said I'll take the Fucking thing, didn't I? Didn't you hear me. It's a car, isn't it? It drives like all the rest. I'll take the damn thing. A 2010 model for $205,000. How can I go wrong?"

"Well, yes Sir. I"

"Get the dam papers ready! Here's my card with my email address. Get the final total over to my office asap, tax and tag included. I'll wire the money over to your office this afternoon. Don't let me down on this ok? Can you handle it?"

"Yes, Sir, I can handle it. Absolutely, Yes Sir and this is your email address."

"I said it was, didn't I?"

"Yes Sir, I'm sorry. I'll rush this through. With full payment, or arranged financing, it should be ready for you by 4:00 at the latest this afternoon."

"OK, let's get this done. I want to drive it to the hotel tonight. My friends will all be there for a big happy hour. "

"Yes Sir. Said the salesman, it's been a pleasure doing business with you."

"Right, Dude. See you at four o'clock."

Heading out the front door of the dealership, Rico climbed into the passenger side of his girlfriend's car.

"Nicole, I got it Baby, I got it. I'm so excited, and that salesman. What a nice guy!"

"Great Rico, will they have it ready today?"

"You bet. We pick it up at 4:00 this afternoon."

"Awesome."

Rico was excited to pick up his new Ferrari.

"We'll be stylin at the big hotel tonight for cocktails."

"Gosh Ricky, honey, we're going to look so good in the Big Red Ferrari tonight. I'm excited too."

"Nicole honey, there are some things I need to take care of this afternoon so, if you don't mind, why don't you just drop me off at the office, then you can go on. That should give you some extra time to get ready for tonight and I'll finish up what I have here to get done. Sound good to you?"

"Sure baby. Do you need me to take you to pick up the car?"

"No, I'll get Carson to take me. Then, I'll be over to pick you up. Oh, say 4:45 be good for you."

"Perfect she said. I'll be ready and waiting."

"You're incredible Nicole. Rico hoped out of the car, shutting the door behind him," he smiled. "See you later."

Chapter Five: BFFL

Jolene Campbell is Beth's best friend. They have known each other since mid-way through their first year of college at FSW. They met, after a baseball game victory celebration in the student union.

Post-game, as the evening progressed, out of the corner of her eye, near the restroom entrance, Jolene noticed a guy who appeared to be getting a little too forward with a girl who she remembered being in her Physiology class. Seeing her discomfort from and the exasperation with the aggressive moves of the overly jealous suiter, Jolene made her way over to where they were engaging and watched.

Finally, she stepped in and told the guy to back off. He ignored her, brushing her aside to get closer to Beth. Jolene turned into him and gave him a big shove. Then, she struck at him hard with her shoulder, like she was tagging a runner out at home plate to keep a winning run from scoring or something.

"Whoa", he said." What's with you?"

Again, he made a quick move to evade her, trying to get closer to Beth.

"That's it Buddy!" Jolene let the guy have it. Like lightning, with an open hand, she mule slapped him up beside his head, catching him between his ear and temple.

Dazed and unsuspecting, he reeled to oppose her.

Instantly, Jolene drop-kicked him hard, upfront and center.

Grabbing hold of each other's hand, Beth and Jolene quickly fled the celebration, leaving the aggressor laying on the floor, moaning, clutching himself below the belt, in the regional vicinity of his family jewels.

Jolene and Beth turned out to be the very best of friends, even rooming together, off campus, for the next three years until graduation.

Sports minded and very athletic, Jolene, like Beth, was a student at FSW. She played as starting catcher for the FSW Women's Softball team. A team to be reckoned with in her Junior and Senior years. Taking the State Championship in 2001 and again in 2002, then went on to play in the NCAA, Women's College World Series, Division I, Championships in Oklahoma City where they finished second. Not what they wanted but still respectable for a small college team effort.

Jolene was white skinned, athletic and sturdily built. At 5'6" tall, weighing 157 pounds she is strong and muscular, without an ounce of fat to be found upon her body. She was fearless in any situation.

Unbeknownst to either of them, each of the two women would ultimately graduate in different fields yet, find themselves working for the same college that they both attended together. Jolene as assistant head coach for the women's FSW softball program, Beth in the Archeology department.

Jolene, being so sports minded, had never been really big on guys. She could usually out play most of them also, so they didn't take much to her either. However, she hadn't given up yet. Coming from a larger family, with two older brothers, she hoped, someday to have kids of her own. I guess you could say she was just a little rough around the edges, but she was very down to earth, witty and sincere. To those she knew and loved, she was fearless and very protective. It was well known throughout the dugout and players at FSW; "You Don't fuck with Momma Bear! She will tear your ass up!" But for the most part she was usually pretty easy going. No one ever called her Joe or Jo Jo either. She preferred to remain rather formal about it all, a family thing, I suppose.

On any typical day you would find Jolene in a cotton, three-button, collared, pullover complete with the FSW Pirate logo on the left shirt breast. Rarely did you see her without her trademark FSW ball cap on with her long, dishwater blond ponytail pulled thru the opening at the back of the hat. Opting for comfort, normally she wore above the knee elastic coaching shorts and shoes that resembled the ones she wore when she used to play, minus the cleats of course.

The friendship that Beth and Jolene had cultivated would prove to last a lifetime for each of them.

Today, Beth rummages through her purse to find her phone. Taps the screen and commanded, "Call Jolene." Instantly the phone acknowledged, "calling Jolene."

Jolene answered, "Hey, how's it going girl?"

"Good, Good Beth, how are you doing today?"

"I'm great Thanks. I was wandering if you can get loose for lunch? I have so much to tell you, you won't even believe it, not to mention I'm already starving this morning. I was thinking around 11:30 ish. At "The Pig", can you make it?"

"You bet." Jolene answered.

"OK, I'll try to get our favorite booth? You will hardly recognize the place, I'm telling you, they've completely remodeled it."

"Really, I had no idea. Sure, I'd love too, thanks for calling. I really need to get out of here for a few hours today. I can just smell that hickory smoke now." Jolene clambered.

"I'll try to get there a couple minutes early. So, do you want me to order us something to drink?" Beth said.

"Great idea, Tall, unsweet Iced Tea, no lemon. Remember?"

"Yep, you got it. Sounds good. See you then."

When Beth arrived at the "Pig Behind the Salad", Jolene was already there.

Beth and Jolene embraced each other with their usual greeting hug with a pretend kiss on either cheek followed by a little shriek of laughter. It's just what they always did.

"Hey, I thought I was going to be the early bird, girlfriend."

"Well, I finished up sooner than I anticipated, and the thought of that BBQ chicken kept calling me. So, I snuck out a little bit early. It's so good to see you."

"You too. Jolene. It's certainly been way too long. Let's not be strangers so much anymore and try to get together more often."

"I agree. Let's do."

"Oh My God! I met the most intriguing guy. His name is Curt Lafferty. He's originally from Oklahoma and now lives in Cape

Coral. When he talks, you can detect just a touch of a southern drawl. Kind of endearing. He's tall and handsome. He has a lot of sandy colored hair on the outside of his forearms. It makes him look so cuddly." Beth smiled.

"So... Have you cuddled with him?"

"No, I only just met him. I hope he calls back soon. I gave him my cell number."

"You gave him your cell number? This sounds serious. I haven't seen you this excited about a guy in years. I thought all that dirt you mess around in had covered up any chance of anything like this ever happening."

"Guess it's still in there I just needed the right stimulus."

"So, what have you been up to?"

"Just playing ball, getting ready for the season. I've got a really good group of girls for the team this year and as always, the higher ups expect us to win. So, we've been putting in a lot of practice hours."

Beth looked to her left. "I'm starving, let's get this show on the road. The salad bar looks great as usual. "

"I'll bet the BBQ is still outstanding too." Jolene said.

"Well, I guess that's why they call it "The Pig Behind the Salad".

"Jolene, what's with the limp? What happened to your leg?"

"Oh, that. Dam near broke my leg. I was giving the new recruits a lesson on how to slide into second base and ended up hurting myself."

"Speaking of a limp, I forgot to tell you. Curt is a retired Apache Helicopter Pilot. When he was over in the Desert Shield conflict in Iraq, his chopper was shot down, His leg was severely broken in the crash. Now he uses a cane to steady his walk. I mean he's not a cripple by any means, but he carries the cane to steady himself."

Interesting. Jolene said. "Beth's got herself a new crippled teddy bear."

"That's not fair Jolene. Curt is every bit the man anyone else I know is. Wait till you see him. I'll bet you change your tune. He's actually built very well and he's over 6 feet tall."

"Ok, I'm sorry. I didn't mean to belittle your new beau. I can't wait to meet him."

"I hope you do too Jolene. Hell, I just hope he calls me back..."

Chapter Six: What Could It Be?

Ohio Jim Hudson, a crusty old man, now in his late 60's. A fisherman who has always made his livelihood trawling the gulf waters from Venice to Ft Myers Beach.

In season, he sets his pots and traps in the sounds for stone crab. Other times he would draw his nets for the annual Whiting run. Otherwise, during the cooler months in Florida, you would find him on his old Trawler, setting the plainer boards deep, pulling mostly at night, for the large & very profitable, White Gulf Shrimp which inhabit the local winter gulf waters off Gasparilla and Cayo Costa Islands.

A transient Floridian, as the name implies, Ohio Jim was born and raised in Cleveland, Ohio. One trip south, while in his teens was all it took. He Pulled up all the stops and headed south to make his home in Florida many years ago.

Jim sports a head of snow-white hair, thinning just a touch up top. Heavy lines accent either side of his, normally squinted, slate blue eyes. His lips are pursed with the normal vertical lines of age, influenced additionally, by many years of smoking.

He still smokes too. "Aint feared", he always says. "After Jennis was taken from me, Hell, A good smoke's all I got left to share my morning cup-a-coffee with."

Jim usually wore a mustache and sported some chin whiskers too. However, these days, I don't think he really gives a dam cause it's all running together. Perhaps he just decided he wasn't going to waste any more money on razors.

Ohio Jim had been married to the same woman for 44 years when the big storm, Charlie, hit the Pine Island area back in 2004. Jim lost his house and his wife and his black lab, Smokey, during that awful storm. His sweet Jennis, the love of his life was taken from him. Jim was caught out near Naples for two days during the storm. Phone lines down, it took him another two days just to get back to where his house had been. He looked for his beloved Jennis for a week, night and day, but he never found her. Smokey neither.

He's still a touch bitter over the whole thing but what's a man to do. Quit living?

He lost his truck too. This is all stuff that country and western songs stem from and are subsequently written about.

Night before last, Jim was pulling his shrimp nets deep thru the waters near Gasparilla island, north of Cayo Costa. At morning light, he and his crew stopped the drag to recover their prize and clear the nets.

As the retrieval winches slowly groaned, the nets raised for clearing, Robert Sanchez, his gaffer, directed Jim to a glint of color at the side of the port trap box. Jim walked around and picked the object up. He stared at it. The look on Ohio Jim's face was of disbelief and amazement for in his hand was what appeared to be a solid gold, escudo sized, some sort of thin coinage. It had some unusual markings on it too.

You know, the thing about gold is when, no matter how long, it's been under water, whether it's been one week or 500 years, it won't corrode and it's still just as shiny as the day it was made, whatever be the case. Jim bit down on the edge of the coin. This coin was definitely gold, or his name wasn't Ohio Jim Hudson.

Jim recalled the local Legend about the Spanish Galleon and the treasure. With the business of making a living and all the ship upkeep, he had all but forgotten about it until that very moment.

He had pretty much always passed it all off as just another story for the weak or easily influenced mind of the tourist. Thinking, like it was an elaborate real estate advertising scheme just to draw people to the area or something.

Yes, that's what he had always thought and that's probably why Gasparilla island was named after the pirate, Jose Gaspar, too. Just another opportunity for retailers and real estate people to enhance the mysticism and allure of the area.

But now, in his hand was food for different thought. He wondered if he was holding what could be confirmed as an item from the treasure of Boca Grande.

"Finders keepers," Jim said to Robert, holding the coin high up over his head. "If it's worth anything I'll let you know."

"Sure, you will Jim. Sure."

Looking up, thru his mind's eye, retracing old times. He remembered that about a month before Hurricane Charlie. He had chanced to meet a young woman at the Yacht Club bar.

Recalling that moment, he remembered her name was Beth. Beth something but, he couldn't recall her last name.

They were both there simply there to have an after workhours cocktail and for some reason, innocently enough, they began talking to each other.

He remembered she worked for FSW and that she was in the Archeology Department. Unusual for a woman, he thought. Jim smiled as he surveyed the opportunity to see her once again. Though there was no love intention, he did remember she was fairly easy to look at.

Jim hoped to find her without too much effort, after all it was a 90-mile round trip from where he now lived on Pine Island. Perhaps, she could shed some light on the find he had made. She may be able to tell him what the origin of the piece was. Maybe, she would identify it, indeed, as a piece of the treasure of Boca

Grande Pass. If it were confirmed to be part of the treasure, there could be more.

Tilting his head, looking up he thought back to the previous night's pull. He remembered his nets dragging roughly for a few feet near the mouth of the pass. Interestingly enough, that's right where legend had always placed the sinking of the old Spanish treasure ship. A big smile grew on Jim's face.

"That's it," he thought, early the next day he would make the trip over across the bridge to the Ft. Myers campus of FSW and try to look her up.

"Who knows?" He thought. "Tomorrow might change my life forever."

Chapter Seven: Through the Woods and Over the Bridge

Wednesday morning came early for Ohio Jim. With the trip to Ft Myers on his mind, he did not rest well throughout the night.

"No reason to lay in bed thinking the days outcome would change with another 15 minutes of sleep." He thought.

Jim sat up on the edge of the bed and stretched. Shakily, he made it to his feet and shuffled into the kitchen where he proceeded to make a pot of coffee. A cup of coffee and a honeybun is about all he ever eats for breakfast anymore. He's never been much of a health buff. Just "fly and get by" is kind of his more recent motto. Carbs and protein are normally not included in his vocabulary, much less his diet.

When Jennis was alive, the mornings were the best time of the day for Jim. They began each day greeting each other with a smile and a hug. Then she cooked breakfast and packed a lunch for him. Each morning, they shared time sitting at the table, content just to be in each other's company.

Each morning, glancing at the clock on the stove, he'd make the same comment. "Well, I guess it's about that time." Then, she'd send him off to the sea with a sack of food, a big hug and a word of encouragement. Theirs's was a wonderful relationship. Each other's sole continually leaning upon the other for support and existence. This co-dependent relationship was, indeed, a healthy one and much appreciated, one to the other. They never had children, but they always had each other.

This morning, he sat there alone at the table for a few moments, sipping on his coffee, watching the smoke rise from his cigarette. He felt the urge to call out to Jennis. But he knew she wouldn't answer him.

He took the soft dishtowel from above the sink and rubbed the coin affectionately. Amazing! The luster increased into a major reflective brilliance. Opening his mouth wide, from the back of his throat, he gently coughed out a breath of moist air over the coin, effectively fogging it. Once again, he applied the polish rag to bring it back to an incredible luster.

He laid the coin down on the table, smiled, crushed out his cigarette in the ash tray which lay beside pepper shaker on the table, turned around and headed towards the back of the house.

Walking into the bathroom, looking into the mirror, he saw the old man standing there staring back at him. "Where's that kid that use to greet me here each morning? Long gone I guess buddy. Lone Gone for sure."

Jim turned the hot water lever and waited for it to come around, then flipped the cold-water handle on to make the stream useable. Cupping his hands to trap the running water, he closed his eyes. With one practiced motion, he splashed the cool water up onto his forehead. Very refreshing, it felt good. He rubbed it down to his chin, then squeegeed it from his face with his long thin fingers.

"I guess I'd better clean this beard up a bit too, out of respect to Beth and all." Jim thought.

He lathered up and proceed to shave with an unsteady hand. Then, splashed on the Skin Bracer. It had been a while since he had felt the sting of an after-shave lotion upon his face.

"I guess I'd better wear something a little better than what I'd wear to the boat too." He said to himself.

"I doubt Beth would appreciate me showing up at her office looking like a bum off the street."

"I hope she remembers me. He said out loud. "Son of a Bitch", that'd be awkward for sure."

"Let's see. These cargo pants look pretty good and this Guayabera shirt is about the best I got so... Well, they say yellow is a happy color, so this will have to do. Sandals are the only shoes I own so I've got no choice there."

Returning to the kitchen, grabbing his favorite insulated roadie cup, he took the handle of the steaming coffee pot then filled the cup to the brim. It was a long drive and most likely, it would take more than the standard coffee fill he was used to each day, to make it all the way over across the big bridge and on over to the FSW campus in Ft Myers.

Jim made his way to the door and pushed the screen open, then turned, shut and locked the door. Like always, he stepped back to allow the spring-loaded screen door to slam shut.

During this time of year everything is covered with heavy dew. Thick pungent smells radiated from the damp matted foliage under his feet, some from the canopy above. Smelling somewhat of dirt and flowers at the same time. Unusual smells to awaken the senses to say the least. Jim loved it though. Cries from local birds, mostly jays and mockingbirds echoed from the branches all around him. Nearby plants and the palms overhead drooped slightly due to the extra weight of the water droplets balancing delicately upon the leaves and fronds.

Just as he stepped off the porch. "DAMMIT! I forgot the dam coin. I'll swear, age is catching up with me."

He turned, re-opened the door and went back inside to retrieve the coin. Exiting once again, he locked the house as before then headed over to his truck.

The rusty chrome door handle was wet and cold as it always was each morning.

Upon opening the door, he was greeted with a familiar loud pop from where the hinge of the driver door was slightly ajar.

Reaching inside, he grabbed a piece of old dish towel and wiped down the outside of the front windshield. Just a little insurance. His wipers didn't work that well at all. But the sun would be completely up soon, and all that moisture would burn off, most likely, by the time he hit Matlacha bridge.

Jim twisted the key and the motor in the old truck slowly rattled to life. He turned on the head lights, put the truck in gear and headed down the path that led to Stringfellow road, then onwards, towards the mainland.

Time behind the wheel that morning passed quickly, not really thinking much about his mission, more like being in a trance than anything else. Thirty-five minutes later, he made the left hand turn off of Del Prado onto the Cape Coral Parkway that lead to the big causeway bridge. Ft Myers and the FSW Campus was now just a few miles away.

Lighting another cigarette, he rolled his window down a touch allowing the exhaled smoke to escape from the cab. Jim coughed a few times but gathered his composure quickly. That cough was becoming a frequent visitor of late but, Jim never gave it a second thought.

The water below the bridge was calm today. What a beautiful sight. With wings fully spread, Pelicans flew close to the structure then glided down within a foot or so of the water.

Ground Effect Gliding was what it was called, pressurizing air between their wings and the water's surface and the pelicans had it down to a science.

On the east side now, just past the Starbucks, Jim turned into the college grounds at the entrance with the big Pirate logo and neon FSW. Following the signs, he found the faculty parking lot and stopped.

Like from out of a movie, Jim looked up to see, none other than Beth Higgins herself right in front of him, heading towards her office. Ohio Jim stuffed out the cigarette against the snuffer bar in the ash tray on the dash. Jumping out of the truck he hollered.

"Beth. Waving," he yelled. " Beth, once again."

Beth turned with a puzzled look upon her face.

"Beth, my name is Ohio Jim, do you remember me?"

"Well, yes. Yes, I do. What in the world are you doing here?"

"Beth, I'm sorry, I forgot your last name."

"Higgins, It's Beth Higgins," she said.

"Yes, Beth Higgins. I'm sorry, I just couldn't remember."

"That's quite alright. Don't worry about it."

"Miss Higgins, I doubt that you remember but, I'm a fisherman. The day before yesterday, we had pulled all night long for shrimp. When we stopped to clear the nets, we found something caught in the corner of the trap box. Is there someplace where we can talk? Someplace private where I can show you what we found."

"Why, sure, my office is right around this corner. We should have plenty of privacy there. You seem pretty excited; I can hardly wait to see what it is."

"Oh, I think you will be amazed Beth. I know I was."

Beth and Ohio Jim walked around the corner shrub to find to outer door of her office already unlocked.

She pushed on the handle which allowed her access into the building. Turning to look at Jim she said, it's Ok, there are other Professors and staff that have offices here too.

"Oh, OK. I really don't want anyone but you to see what I found. If this gets out it could cause quite a stir."

Beth raised her eyebrows and said, "Really?"

"Oh yah."

Once inside her office, Jim told her about the night and subsequent morning on the shrimp boat. He told her about the planers and about the nets dragging on the bottom at Boca Grande Pass and about the discovery they found in the port clearing trap.

Jim reached into the front pocket of his cargo pants and pulled out the gleaming coin.

With two fingers Jim held it up to the light.

Beth gasped. "Oh My God, that's incredible Jim. Absolutely incredible."

"I thought you'd think so Beth. I'm almost positive it's solid gold. And what's even more amazing, we may have dredged it up exactly where the old Legend of Boca Grande Pass treasure was supposed to have been."

Beth gazed at the coin and then back at Jim with a look of awe and amazement upon her face.

"Can I hold it? Can I look at it more closely? Do you mind?"

"Not at all Beth, that's why I came to see you this morning. I brought this over for you to help me figure out what it is. Here, look at these unusual markings and designs on it."

Beth took the coin in her hand. Carefully, she looked closely at the it. "Yes, they're definitely not Spanish markings." Beth said. "I've seen lots of those. These look more like the markings of early Indians. Maybe South American or such."

Beth quickly handed the coin back to Jim, stood up and turned to see another person standing in the shadow of the hallway to her work room.

"Who's there? YOU THERE! What are you doing in my office? I demand that you come out this instant."

"Ah, it's just me Beth, Professor Alvera said, don't be alarmed."

Visibly upset for the intrusion, very sternly, Beth demanded; "How long have you been standing there? What are you doing in my office?"

"Ah, Only for a few minutes dear. Not long at all. I did not mean to alarm you. Ah, I thought I may have misplaced my notebook here the other day. I had gone into your study hoping to find it."

"My apologies, I'll be on my way now."

Doctor Walter Alvera, associate Professor and understudy to Departmental head, Beth Higgins in the FSW Archelogy dept.

A round-faced man leaning towards the well-fed side, he sports a heavy mustache, bushy eyebrows and a medium to light brown complexion. His hair is dark brown, normally cut short around the ears, it parts naturally in the middle.

Now in his mid-60's, Dr. Alvera has eyesight trending towards farsighted failure even at his early age and is forced to wear, brown framed, under half reading glasses which are usually found at or near the end of his nose. A glasses lanyard hanging around his neck has proven, of late, to be beneficial in keeping up with them in times of need. Hesitant at times, he speaks in an almost Peter Lorre like tone with a slight upper east coast accent.

Professor Alvera left the room via the hall that lead to his own nearby office.

"How did you know he was there Beth? I didn't see or hear a thing."

"I swear to God Jim. I smelled him." Beth said. "Didn't you smell it. He's got some kind of stinky gross odor that follows him around. I smelled him even before I saw him. I knew he was near instinctively, that's why I jumped up and called out to the other room. I hate that smell too. I just can't figure out why he would be in my office this early in the morning, uninvited."

Dr. Alvera works in the same department that Beth heads. Even though he had earned his doctorate in Ancient Science Studies, he missed his chance to become head of the FSW Archelogy department, because of an unfortunate and untimely, artifact appraisal scandal that he was indicated to be involved in at the time promotions were given out. Though Professor Alvera, was not fired from his position at the school, by his own doing he had fallen short of his life's ambition. He would remain openly jealous of Beth in her position for many years to follow.

In Florida, the work force, in many instances, chooses to adopt a very relaxed approach to daily work apparel, like camp shirts, Shorts and flip flops, are all acceptable.

Dr. Alvera, however, still chooses to remain fairly formal in attire and usually wears slacks, traditional leather shoes with dark sox. His navy blue sportscoat exhibits somewhat threadbare elbows, well-worn slick sleeves that cover a short sleeve white cotton shirt. A faint sometimes pungent odor always seems to be detected in his presence. Perhaps it's due to poor self-hygiene. Some say a good trip to the dry cleaners might remedy the matter. Others blame it on poor bathing habits. At any rate, sometimes his presence is detected prior to his personal arrival.

"Stinky Man is what some of the students call him. Smarmy maybe a better word. Obviously, he struggles with unclean demons' other than just those he finds in ancient graves."

Meanwhile, he continues to work at FSW. He remains hopeful that another opportunity will come for him. One that will allow him to prosper further than his College salary. Meanwhile, he teaches class at the College and keeps under the radar of most of the other faculty.

With a flawless record, exceptional grades and two life achievement awards to go with them, Elizabeth Higgins was made Departmental head instead.

Dr. Walter Alvera never seemed much of a concern to Beth as she was seldom confined to the offices on campus. The two rarely if ever crossed paths.

"Dammit Jim, I apologize to you for that intrusion. Beth exclaimed. I have no idea how long he was standing there or what, if anything he heard us talking about."

"Don't worry about it. It's like everything else in life Beth. Nothing is forever, and secrets seldom hold their celebrity for long. Let's just hope he didn't hear us talking about this."

"Ok, back to the artifact. Do you mind if I take some pictures of this coin and do some research on it? That's the only way I'm going to be able to help you with this mystery."

"Sure, sure, sounds good to me. Nothing like writing a new Sherlock Holmes episode to make life more interesting. Right Beth?"

"You nailed it Jim. This is amazing. I hope it proves to be something really good for you."

"Jim, I know nothing about you. I don't even have you phone number. So, if you don't mind, take this notebook and write down some info on how I can get ahold of you. It will take me at least a couple of days to find out anything on this. Then I'll get back to you on it."

"Jim took the notebook. He wrote upon it his Pine Island address and phone number, then handed it back to her."

"Thanks for helping me with this Beth. This could be big."

"Hey, You're welcome. This is what I thrive on Jim. Mysteries of old."

"Beth, just a quick question before I go. Let's say this is from the time of the Legend, I'm almost positive it's solid gold. Do you have any idea how much something like this might be worth?"

Oh, wow Jim, your coin isn't Spanish but, a Spanish Escudo or Piece of Eight, as they are called, the same size, depending upon its condition, is worth between $75,000 to $90,000 dollars."

"Are you kidding me? $90,000 dollars?"

Jim, you should be careful about telling anyone where it came from because there are treasure leases and federal claims all around the coastal waters in Florida that are still in place. I'll try to find some information on that for you too."

"Thank You so much Beth. It's been great seeing you again. I appreciate all of your help."

"Absolutely." Beth said. "Mysteries of the earth are my life. Sometimes they show up at the darndest times just begging for an explanation. By the way, I'd put that somewhere it's safe till we figure all this out Jim."

"Oh, I will Beth. I've got just he place for it."

Beth walked Jim to her office door. I'll call you as soon as I have some information for you. Your car is around the corner to the left in the parking lot."

"Thanks again Beth. I'll talk to you soon."

Jim opened the door and walked towards the outside entrance. On his left as, he passed down the hall, he saw Professor Alvera, standing in the unlit doorframe of his office. His arms gently folded. Dr. Alvera smiled a slight smile and nodded his head downwards as Jim passed.

Jim tipped his head briefly in return, then went on towards the exit. "Yep, there's that dam smell again. Just like Beth said. How could that be good for the students? That guy gives me the creeps anyway he thought."

By the time Jim hit the outside door he already had his lip loaded with a cigarette. The lighter in his other hand lit and swinging up to light it. Awe...Jim thought. "Way past time for a smoke." Jim took a drag and inhaled it as deeply as he could. The taste was right. Just like an old friend, always there to greet and comfort him.

Opening the door of his truck, he hopped in, turned the key and made the loop out of the parking lot. Time for lunch, he thought. Guess I'll stop at Five Guys. It's been awhile since I had a good burger and fries.

Later that afternoon, Professor Alvera made his way back over to Beth's office, stuck his head in the door and knocked. Banging lightly with his finger knuckles, "Ah, Knock Knock," he said.

"Professor Alvera, what is it? What can I do for you?"

"Ah, Doctor Higgins, I owe you an apology, I should have waited until you were in your office before I looked for my notebook. I am, Ah, so sorry for the intrusion this morning, please forgive me."

"I'll overlook it this time Professor Alvera but, I am asking you to stay out of my office when I'm not here. Besides, you scared the heck out of me."

"Ah, yes, it was most embarrassing for me also, I am terribly sorry." "I found the notebook at lunch, in the front seat of my car. How clumsy of me."

"It happens." Beth muttered, somewhat put out by the intrusion.

"Ah, so what do you think Dr. Higgins?"

"Think? Think about what?"

"What that man was talking to you about?"

"Professor Alvera, I have no idea what you are talking about. The thing he had was no more than a trinket to be found in a cereal box. He did nothing more than take up my precious time."

"Let's let this be the end of our conversations about this? It goes no further, Understand?"

"Ah, yes Mam. Sorry, I'll take my leave now."

"Good day, Professor Alvera!"

Beth returned to her mornings work.

* * *

Chapter Eight: What's in Your Salad

Just a year ago they met on the boardwalk at south beach. When Rico first saw Nicole, she was enjoying an ice cream cone, walking on the pier near the Yacht Club. He had always been somewhat of an opportunist where women are concerned, how could he miss this chance. This Chick is rocket fuel material and she was headed straight for the moon. Rico surveyed the situation as he decided on his next move. Such the charming salesman, he walked straight up to her and introduced himself. It must have been the big smile he possessed or his Aire of confidence because the two have been all but inseparable since.

Nicole Newsome, of Newsome family fame in Southern Florida. A stunningly attractive young woman... Ten years the junior to Enrique. Tan as a muffin at a bake sale, she stands 5'6" tall. Like an athletic angel with long flowing dark brown hair. Long black eyelashes outline her big brown eyes that seemingly cast a smile in every direction.

Nicole's adolescent years were filled with sports activities during school. An accomplished soccer player, she played for the intermural Miami Sharks. While her legs exhibit solid muscular development, she is thin waisted, often wearing shirts that reveal her midriff. Sports abs compliment an artistically carved stomach. Her breasts are of noticeable size and as may be expected for a 21-year-old, she doesn't mind showing them off wearing collarless, low cut, V neck shirts of color. Short shorts and sandals usually, finish out her leisure dress of the day.

Her dad owns the Tampa Bay Tarpon, pro football team. Nicole had always had most everything she's wanted and why not? She's a beautiful girl and she knows just how to play the men she's around, including Rico. The Tarpons remain undefeated. They continue to play hard while hoping for another great season this year. Though they have never won the super bowl, they've been to the playoffs twice previously.

Rico always gets a big reaction from Nicole when he asks how her dad's football team, the Tampa Bay Tampons, is doing. Then she reacts and throws a complete fit. Acting mad and hurt, turning away from him. Naturally, he follows her, apologizes, gives her a big hug and a kiss. Then makes up to her swearing he'll never say it again. Afterwards it's off to have more fun with feelings mended. It's become kinda of a game for them that sometimes leads later to the catalyst of what usually holds a relationship together.

The email and attachment to finalize the deal on the car came into Rico's office from the dealership at 1:30 that afternoon. Rico opened the attachment which accompanied the email.

"Son of a Bitch, that's fucking robbery. The price for the car was $205,000.

Going down the list he read:

"6% Sales tax: $12,300,

1% County sales tax: $2,050,

Registration by weight fee: $70.65,

64

Registration base fee $225.00,

License plate transfer fee: $7.65,

Base title fee: $75.25.

Total $219,728.55."

"Son of a bitch, that's insane. Everybody's got their fucking hand out. I understand on the sales tax but the rest of this is a crock of shit."

He took a moment to calm down before calling the bank to make the arrangements for the money to be wired to the dealership. He hoped to clear the car for this afternoon's pickup.

"Hello, Central Bank, Ms. Pearsall here, how may I help you?"

"Jennifer, Enrique Ribeiro here, how are you dear?"

"Rico, I'm just fine and certainly better now that you've called. Where have you been, I haven't heard from you lately?"

"Sorry. Working Dear. Working. Business is booming, Jennifer."

"Well, I certainly understand that. I guess I was just getting my feelings hurt for nothing. I know you're busy. What can I do for you today dear?"

"I bought a car this morning over at Main South Ferrari of Miami and I need to get some money over there via wire asap. Just deduct it from my business account."

"I'm just the gal to talk to about this and I'll certainly get it done for you. By the way, when you catch a break, I'll take you up on your drink offer at South Beach Yacht Club. It could turn out to be fun."

"You bet dear; I'm completely covered up right now. But I'll give you a call as soon as the workload eases up a bit."

"Wonderful, Rico, do you have the bank routing number for the dealership?"

"Tell you what, I'm just going to forward the invoice from the dealership including all payment instructions to you, so nothing goes wrong. I'm supposed to pick it up at 4:00 this afternoon."

"Ok, Rico darling. I'll take care of it all and email you once it's completed. Thank You so much and don't keep me waiting so long next time. I'll look forward to our rendezvous. Bye Bye dear."

It's just something in his blood, I guess. No attractive single women is ever safe from his advances. Like the old Rickey Nelson song, he's got one in every port. Guess he wanted to taste a little sample of them all. After all, why not? He's young and exceptionally handsome. Looking back though, none of the women on his list had ever complained after he moved on.

Meanwhile back at Rico's office. "Carson, did that package from Egypt make it through?"

"Yes, Sir. I believe this is it. The one with the crazy writing on the label."

"Great, Un-crate it when you get a chance. I want those items transferred into the Columbian coffee tins as soon as you can. I don't want to take a chance on loosing this sale. I'll probably hear from the buyer by tomorrow. I want them ready for delivery the moment we get the call. Now that I think of it; put the box they came in into the incinerator too."

"Yes, Sir, I'll take care of that. No problem. I'll make it vanish completely."

"Great. Carson, once more thing, before too long, would you mind running me down to Main South Miami Ferrari. I have something there I need to pick up."

"Sure, I'll be glad to. Let me give this to the girls up front to finish for me and we'll be off."

"Thanks Buddy, I'll meet out back by your truck."

Shortly thereafter, they took off for Main South Ferrari.

"Mr. Enrique!"

"The name's Ribeiro. Enrique Ribeiro."

"I'm terribly sorry Sir. I normally don't have recall problems like this. Please forgive me. We received the wire transfer and everything is set. Here is your title, No Lien, your new plates, all your registrations and most importantly, the keys to your Ferrari."

"Sounds good. Everything all together ready to go. I hate loose ends. Thanks Dude. She looks great."

"Thank You Sir. I had the guys in the shop give it the Once over. Everything's perfect under the hood and they put a shiny coat of wax on it for you."

"For that price I deserve nothing less."

For some reason, that salesman brought out the mean streak in Rico. Sometimes he can be a complete jerk, the behavior he was currently exhibiting, being the prime example.

Rico took the keys and headed for the car. With a twist of his wrist the Ferrari roared to life. The smooth sound of Ferrari power escaped through the twin chrome pipes from behind the car. A big smile came over his face as he put the car in gear to exit the dealership. Rock and Roll he thought. Let's Rock and Roll. Powering up to shift into second gear, he headed over to first street then down the causeway towards Nicole's house. It was 4:35, he could make it to her house in ten minutes with good traffic.

When Rico rolled up to Nicole's house, she was waiting outside.

"I filmed you driving up to my house just now. The car is unbelievable she gleamed. She jumped into the front seat leaned over and kissed him on the cheek. Let's do this," she said.

Raising the motors RPM's for sound effects, then aggressively letting out on the clutch, they departed loudly so everyone could hear. Rico and Nicole headed towards the Fountain Blue.

Traffic was normal for Miami at 4:50pm. It was then that he suddenly realized he was driving his new Ferrari in a sea of $3000 - dollar automobiles and that no one cared how much his car cost.

"Shit, he thought, hope those bastards stay in their own fucking lanes. I hate this. I almost need my own highway."

Upon arrival, he rolled into valet area to park. "Ok buddy, a twenty-dollar bill to you if you let me back this thing up right here in front."

"Sure Mister. Knock yourself out."

Rico backed the Ferrari into the prime hotel valet parking spot, got out and flipped the keys to the Valet attendant." No one touches the car. No one, understand?"

"Yes Sir, not even me. Nice car, I'll keep an eye on it for you."

Rico exited the car then quickly skirted to the passenger side where he opened the door, extending his hand to Nicole. She stepped out of the crimson carriage as if she was entering a play center stage, smiling to her right then to her left. Everyone nearby watched intently as Rico's shiny accomplice walked confidently through the parking area.

As they reached the main entrance, the sliding glass doors of the hotel opened automatically where they were greeted with a blast of cold air hitting them in the face. Through the lobby and over to the bar area, Rico looked in the direction of the table they usually haunted. Two of Rico's buddies waved them over towards them. Their girlfriends were deep in conversation and didn't notice when they arrived.

"Hey, Hey! We heard you scored a new ride dude."

"Oh Wow! How'd you find that out?" Rico blurted.

"Marilynn talked to Nicole this afternoon. Now it's all over town."

"Figures. Nicole Honey, what will you have? The usual ok?"

"OK, bring her a white wine spritzer and I'll have a Vodka martini. I'd like two big olives. Make it dirty and shake chill it twice. I'll need a pepper shaker and two bar napkins please."

Rico's cell phone rang just as the drinks arrived at the table. Annoyed at the disturbance, he looked to see who the caller was.

"Excuse me, I have to take this. Hello, Mrs. Molenkamp, how are you doing today?"

"Oh, Rico darling, I just couldn't wait till tomorrow to call you. Is everything still on?"

"Yes, Mam. It's all good."

"My husband and I had just one question, are you firm at $180,000?"

"That's what we had talked about, isn't it?"

"Well, yes but I was wondering. Would entertain an offer of, say $165,000? I will bring a big bag of Cash-ews to sweeten the deal."

Picking up on the makeshift play on words. "So, you're talking a straight green salad with pure U.S. dollarmo dressing?" Rico replied.

"Yes, I am. No questions asked."

"You know Mrs. Molenkamp; I think we can agree on that for the three salads. Will you be picking them up tomorrow?"

"If it's quite convenient she replied."

"Very well then, I look forward to seeing you, shall we say your office, in the morning around 10:30."

"My husband and I will be there and Thank You so much."

"You are certainly welcome. Thank You."

Rico hung up the phone as he reached for his drink. No loose ends here he thought.

"You know guys, America's a great country, when you don't have to deal with the little people. I do love it so."

Chapter Nine: Loose Lips Sink Ships.

"Hello, Ah, Mr. Ribeiro. Ah, I'd like to speak to Mr. Enrique Ribeiro please. Tell him it's Professor Walter Alvera, Ah, he knows who I am."

"Yes Sir, will you please hold."

"Ah, Certainly. Thank You."

"Rico, Line two. I could barely hear this guy. He says it's Professor Walter Alvera."

"Ok, thanks, I'll take it in my office. Will you shut the door please?"

"Hello, Rico here."

"Hello Rico, ah, this is, Professor Alvera in Ft Myers."

"Dr. Alvera, what have you been up these days? It's been quite a while since we've heard from you."

"Ah, yes, it's been a while for sure. You are well, I trust?"

"Couldn't be better Professor. The world is treating me just fine. Tell me, to what do I owe the honor of this call."

"Rico, Ah, the last time we talked, you said that if I ran across anything interesting, that you, Ah, would make it worth my while if I gave you a call."

"Yes, I remember."

"Well, Ah, something came up earlier in the day that I thought that you may be interested in. Ah, something that may be worth an extraordinary amount of money."

"Keep talking man, you've got my attention."

"Well, Ah, today before classes began, a stranger came to FSW to see the departmental head, Beth Higgins."

"He was an older, white headed man. I'd never seen him before. He said he was a fisherman."

"Ah, anyway, I was in her study looking for a notebook that I had misplaced, when they came into her office. It was very awkward. I was trapped there with no way to exit her office so, I, ah, remained in the shadows of her study."

"This guy proceeded to show her some sort of coin or artifact, he said he had found when he was trawling for shrimp in the gulf a few days ago. They both agreed it was solid gold. It was about the size of a Spanish Piece of Eight. They talked about it as if it could relate to a number of different possibilities. Ah, mainly, his question to Dr. Higgins was if she thought that the coin might confirm the old Legend of the Treasure of Boca Grande."

"Treasure, you say."

"Ah, Yes, Legend has it that around 500 years ago a Spanish ship was sunk by a Calusa war party at the mouth of Boca Grande Pass. The ship that supposedly sank there was full of artifacts, treasure, trunks of gold and silver. I know of the Legend. Though the mystery of it still circulates in the area, up until now, there has never been much of anything found to confirm or deny it to be an event that ever, actually took place."

"While they talked, it was all I could do to remain quiet. I must have made a noise or something because Dr. Higgins sensed my presence, then called me out from behind the study wall before I could learn any more. It was very embarrassing when she asked me how long I had been standing there. Then she told me sternly to leave."

"Afterwards, I tried to hang out as close to her office door as I could but, she shut it for privacy. I couldn't hear much past that point."

"Where is the coin now Professor? Did he keep it or does Doctor Higgins have it?"

"Ah, well, I think she took pictures of it to research but, I believe he took the coin with him. So, before we go any further, I'd like to know. Can I count on my normal fee and cut if this information proves to be of value.?"

"Professor Alvera, I have never shanked you. Have I?"

"Well, no, you never have but, this may prove to be a much larger deal than the last few that we have been involved in together. Perhaps upwards around $800 to $900 million dollars."

"$900 Million dollars. Son of a Bitch! Now you're talking. Oh My God, unbelievable."

"Don't worry about it Professor. Get me more information. Help me. Find out all you can, and I'll make sure you're the richest man at FSW. Don't worry Professor, I'll make sure you get everything that you have coming to you."

"Ah, very well then. I'll see what I can do."

"There is one more thing Rico. I remember, he said his name was Ohio Jim."

"Rico, are you interested in trying to make a deal to buy the coin? If so, I'll try to find out where he resides."

"Good deal Professor Alvera, find out all you can, and I'll take it from there."

"Ah, Yes, I will do just that. I'll get back to you as soon as I have anything."

"Work quickly Professor, Things like this have a way of finding their way out of the bag. I don't want this to get away from us."

"Ah, Yes, I'm on it Rico. I'm on it! As he hung up the phone."

Rico hung up also.

Practically, within the same breath; "Brenda, get Melvin Swift at the Pine Island commercial dock on the phone. See if he's ever heard of a fisherman who goes by the name Ohio Jim. I want to know where this guy lives."

"Certainly, Mr. Ribeiro. Right-a-way."

"NOW, Brenda! I want it now!"

"Yes Sir! I'm on it."

Mid-Point Dock on Pine Island was a specialized area, strictly used by commercial fisherman, crabbers and bait hunters. It's located just a mile south of Center Junction.

Melvin Swift had worked as controller of the dock for the past 16 years. He lived on Pine island too. If anyone knew who Ohio Jim was, he would.

"Mr. Ribeiro, I spoke with Melvin Swift just know."

"Yes and..."

"He does know a man named Ohio Jim. He said Ohio Jim lives up north on Pine Island near Bokeelia. He said his house is located north, just past the last Palm Tree farm, then left on down to the end of the dirt road. He gave me his Telephone number too. Would you like it?"

"Yes, give it to me and...not a word about this to anyone. Do You Understand? Rico said emphatically. Not a Word!"

Chapter Ten: Columbia Calling

After she had finished her morning coffee, Beth pulled some books from the library shelves. She shuffled through the pages hoping to identify the markings on the coin that Jim had shown her. It took the better part of the morning, thumbing through a number of books, looking at all the illustrations they contained. One contained a write-up on the Muisca Indians of Columbia There, she found the exact mark that was upon the coin. It was most definitely a Muisca marking.

Beth spent the rest of the afternoon looking through the International College/University directory, South America, in hopes of finding someone she could enlist to help identify and date the coin that Ohio Jim had shown her.

She found an Emeritus Professor, Dr. Miguel Rodriquez Fuentes, with the Universidad Nacional de Colombia de Los Andes. Now retired, he still consults as former head of studies of Archeology and in the Early Eastern Highland people's research. He is an authority on the Muisca Indians and speaks the ancient language of Chibcha.

Believing this was an excellent place to start, Beth, tore through her files looking for the Form Letter that would make it all official. She wrote out an appropriation request, an "Order of Approval", to present to the FSW President for clearance to make some International phone calls. Beth took the request personally to the University office in an attempt to have it quickly approved and signed.

Upon entering the campus administrative offices, Beth encountered Dr. William Anderson, Dean of FSW Geological Sciences. Beth talked to him at length telling him of the possibilities of a great find and asking for his indulgence to approve and fund the phone calls to South America. Beth showed him a picture of the coin she hoped to gain information on.

Knowing Beth well, that she was straight lined, very dedicated to fossil and archeological record and as a former student of his, Dr. Anderson was intrigued with her excitement and all that Beth had to say. Dr. Anderson signed the Form of Approval, not to exceed $350, sealed it and handed it back to Beth. With great excitement, Beth headed towards the door taking the Approval Form with her. Over her shoulder, she told Dr. Anderson, she would keep him informed.

"Please do," Dr. Anderson replied

After lunch, Beth consulted the International Directory once again. Finding the Overseas telephone number for Dr. Fuentes, she logged in the approval FSW codes and placed the call. After an hour and a half, the call finally went through to Columbia.

Upon his answering, Beth respectfully, introduced herself. Once the formalities of the phone meeting were finalized, Beth began to tell the story to Dr. Fuentes. She described the artifact that had been found nearby by the Old Fisherman in his nets. She told him that she was attempting to confirm an old legend about a sunken Spanish ship that sank years ago and that the coin might be a part of the cargo that the sunken ship had carried on board.

She said she had identified the markings as Muisca Indian. Hence, the reason for her call to him. She asked Dr. Fuentes some questions about the Muisca Indians of the Eastern Highlands. About their plight in and around 1517- 1519 and if there was any documented history regarding them during that time.

Beth expressed to Dr. Fuentes that she felt that any information acquired had to come from that exact time in order to tie them at all to the missing treasure and confirm the legend. She emailed Dr. Fuentes a full color photo of the coin asking him to identify it if he could.

On their second call, two days later, Dr. Fuentes filled Beth in on all that he had learned.

"To begin with," Dr. Higgins said, "I believe this coin and others like it, helped to create the legend of "El Dorado". The markings on the coin are the sign of the Muisca Guatavita goddess. It became linked to the Muiscas and their famous Laguna de Guatavita. The origin of the legend was located in the central Muisca Confederation of Columbia."

"A member of the Muisca priesthood, known as the Zipa, would wear a ritual mask and gold covered clothing in dance, then offer to the Guatavita Goddess gold and other treasures."

"This ritual was to gain notoriety and fuel the Rumors of El Dorado which caused the Spanish conquest of Columbia. The country that was named after Christopher Columbus, even though he had never set foot on Columbian soil. Columbus had, however, previously explored the Sierra Nevada de Santa Marta and was astonished by the wealth of the local Indians."

"The gold they possessed and their stories about fabulous treasures inland all helped to give rise to the myth of "El Dorado", a mysterious kingdom abundant in gold."

"In its most extreme interpretation, El Dorado was believed to be a land of gold mountains littered with emeralds."

"From the moment the Spaniards arrived, their obsession with "El Dorado" became the principal force driving them into the interior. Digging deeper into another accounting of events; It is documented that in 1518, in the east Andes, the northern confederation, on the upper eastern most highlands of the Muisca territory, a massacre of two Muisca Indian villages did occur at the hands of the Spanish Conquistadores or Spanish fighters as they were called in the notes."

"Other villages and settlements in the same surrounding area were pillaged for their wealth also. Historical recordings reveal that the Spanish then headed out of the region northwards, towards Central America. It is unknown exactly how much treasure was taken but it was said to have been considerable."

"Dr. Fuentes, the date you mentioned of 1518 coincides exactly with the date given for the sinking of the Spanish ship, the Nuestra Senora de Madrid. That could go a long way to confirming that the legend is true.", Beth said excitedly.

"So then, our efforts have been worthwhile. Recorded historical research, once again proves that it is not unlike working an archeological concession; the more we dig, the more we uncover."

"I totally agree Dr. Fuentes. You are marvelous. I appreciate you so much. There are not enough words for me to Thank You."

"Very well then Professor Higgins. I'll assume that you will keep me in the loop as to any progress that you make concerning all of this."

"Absolutely, Dr. Fuentes, without a doubt! Thank You so much."

Beth wished Dr. Fuentes well, then hung up the phone. She couldn't wait to call Ohio Jim. There was much work to be done.

Chapter Eleven: We Can Do This

It had been almost a week since the chance meeting between Curt and Beth at Starbucks. Today, Beth was busily cleaning and re-organizing her office. She really hadn't had time to put it back in shape since she returned from the last dig, she was overseeing near Lake Okeechobee.

Her office seemed to always be cluttered with stacks of scientific literature, books, technical devices and or analytical equipment of some sort. The main, research desk towards the back of her office remained inundated with the artifacts she was currently studying, dirt and plaster dust. Very messy for a woman who prided herself in her organizational abilities. Such a fine line to walk to maintain a balance between being tidy or trending towards complete clutter.

As Beth picked up a tall stack of books near the research table, the phone rang. Looking around the books, straining a bit, she navigated her way between the obstacles, hoping to stop the incessant ringing of the phone. Picking up the receiver; "Arch Lab, Beth Higgins", Can I help you?"

"Hello, Beth. This is Curt, Curt Lafferty."

"CURT! HI!" She answered excitedly, "What a pleasant surprise." Allowing her attention to her task to momentarily lapse, the entire stack of books crashed to the floor. Beth's elation over hearing Curt's voice was evident also in her smile.

"What was that?" Curt said very concerned.

"Oh nothing, just an a stack of old books fell over, that's all."

"Wow, that musta been a big stack of books. Beth, I hope you don't mind me calling you at your office. I..."

"No, No Curt, Not at all. How are you?"

"I'm great thanks. I was just calling to invite you to an outdoor BBQ cook out at my house this coming Saturday afternoon. Ribs, chicken, baked beans and potato salad. I'm having a couple of my Cape Coral friends over too and I was wondering. Do you think you can make it?"

"Saturday eh? What time are you thinking Curt?"

"Well, I'm going to start cooking around noon before the Dolphins game, but I have to go to the store a little bit earlier to do some shopping for the day. If you can come over, say around eleven, I was thinking you could meet Bandit and perhaps go to the store with me. I mean if you wouldn't mind helping me."

"Sure, I think I can handle that. Matter of fact. I'd love too. What's the dress?"

"Why, Florida of course. Shorts, shirt and flippies. What else? It's a deal then? My address is 5224 Tomer Drive, Cape Coral, 33904. See you at eleven O'clock Saturday morning."

"Ok, I'll be there."

"Awesome, see you then."

Beth hung up the phone, smiled and sat down in the chair behind her desk. Why did she feel so elated? Why did she feel so giddy, so anticipatorily nervous? These feelings that stirred inside of her were indicative of more than just a friendship.

Friends don't make friends nervous. Friends don't make people feel like they were just given a week's free pass to Disney World. No there is something more here she thought. Once again, the recollection of that peculiar odor she remembered smelling when she was next to Curt entered her mind. It all seemed so pleasurable, so inviting, so easy to be near.

Curt hung up the phone. Smiling, he pumps his fist and yells; "Alright! I was So, hoping she could make it. I can't wait. This is going to be fun."

"What shall I do?" Beth thought. Saturday seems such a long way off. This is only Thursday. Right now, that seems like a lifetime. But I know the time will pass quickly. Why did she feel so anxious? It reminded her of when she was a child and her daddy promised to take her to ride the Shetland ponies, next to the root beer stand on the weekend. Then, having to deal with all of the uneventful days in between waiting. It was just too much time to deal with for a girl who was so full of life.

Throughout the rest of the day, Beth found herself unable to focus on the tasks she had at hand. Frequently, she drifted off into the land of this new man she had met. Into a place of excitement and fantasy, where her spirits soared like an Osprey flying on high. She felt...so alive. It had been such a long time since Beth could remember feelings like the ones she was now experiencing. It was a wonderful thing.

"Be still my heart", she told herself, as she gracefully danced about the office floor. It was indeed exciting. But for now, she took a deep breath and reminded herself. "No Expectations. Let it unfold as fate would have it. We must protect ourselves and remain patient. After all, this could be just another emotional dead end. No way!", She thought. "There's something to this. She could feel it and you know what they say about a woman's intuition."

Saturday morning came around right on time as scheduled. Beth rose early. A nice bath, wash my hair, do my toenails. There was so much to do. Now she worried that it would be hard to fit it all in before the agreed arrival time.

Punctual as always though, Beth arrived at Curt's house at five till eleven. Completely unlike her, she never even checked the address upon seeing the gun metal gray Jeep in the driveway proving that directions are worthless once the objective is in sight. She parked in the drive, walked up to the front screen and rang the doorbell. Curt, quickly, came to the door. He greeted her with a slight hug and exclaimed; "It's great to see you again Beth. Welcome to my home. Curt took a step back to look at her. What a cute shirt that is."

"Oh, you like it. Thanks. It's my signature print Camp Shirt. I like the collar and I always have to have a pocket on my shirt."

"Oh, wow, this is beautiful. You didn't say you had a swimming pool."

"Really Beth, what self-respecting Transient Floridian would have a home in Florida without a swimming pool?"

"Well, you do have a good point there", Beth Agreed.

"And this must be Bandit."

Barking, Bandit pranced up to Beth and licked her hand, as if to welcome her to his home.

"He's wonderful and like you said, he has such a beautiful coat. I don't think I've ever seen a dog like this."

"He's a Blue Healer. Lots of them back in Oklahoma. Pretty common there. Curt said. They work them allot around livestock in the mid-west."

"He's so soft and what a friendly dog."

Bandit left the room, then returned with a tennis ball in his mouth. He makes his way back over to Beth, drops the ball, then lifts his paw as if to shake.

"Bandit, we're not going to get that started. He will wear you out with that tennis ball. I'm not kidding you either. It's like he has unending energy when that yellow ball is in play. Bandit go lay down now and let us get some things done." Instantly obeying, Bandit, quietly turned and walked towards his pad.

"I'm so happy you came over today Beth. It's going to be a wonderful day. Let me put some music on. How about some Donald Fagan, The Night Fly album? Is that good for you?"

"Great, I love his music. Especially, the song "New Frontier."

"Yeah me too, I think my favorite is "The Goodbye Look" though", Curt said. "I actually like all the songs on that album. You know his stuff is over 30 years old, but it still sounds so current and refreshing."

"Yes, I totally agree Curt. What can I help with?" Beth insisted enthusiastically."

"Let's see, you can add that little jar of mustard and stir that potato salad and I'll do the beans, if you like."

"Sure, I'd be glad too. Sure smells good."

"Both are my Mom's recipes and they taste great." Curt replied.

"Ok now, we'll just cover them and put this all in the fridge, then off to the store we'll go."

Curt and Beth walked out the front door and headed towards the driveway.

"Looks like you parked behind me and you know what that means."

" What's that? Curt."

"We have to take your car. " he said laughing. "Wow, it looks brand new."

"Oh, OK, That's fine with me. It is new." She replied.

Curt already had the main meat entrees, hopefully Publix would have everything else he needed. Looking at the list he read: "Two cases of Beer, a big bag of ruffle chips, two 20-pound bags of ice and a bunch of little green onions. Finally, a bottle each of liquid smoke and Lea & Perrins finished off the shopping list. All complete now". He turned the cart towards the payout line. Curt pulled out his American Express, Gold Card and instantly chipped the payment.

"Paper or plastic Sir?"

"Plastic is great by me."

"Ok, Thank You. Replied the sacker."

"There! I think we have everything we need."

Out the front door of the grocery store, they walked together.

"Beth. Did you ever notice there's something about the smells that follow you out of the of a grocery store? It's like the produce department combines with the floral shop and the bakery all at once. When those sliding doors open, there's a cold, sensory overloading wind rushing out from behind that seems to push you out into the blacktop environment of the parking lot. It always has the same peculiar refreshing smell, no matter which store you leave. Coming or going."

"That's Interesting Curt. Beth said smiling. Now that you mention it, I do think it's something for the senses to cling to. Nothing like fond memories of the grocery store." She said. Smiling.

From there on, obviously, both Curt and Beth were completely engrossed in thought because, the only noise that could be heard from the closing sliding glass doors closing behind them, on out to the car, was the popping sound of the uneven wheel on the shopping cart.

Beth hit the button on the key fob to unlock the car doors. Curt pushed the cart around, reached over and lifted the rear hatch of the new Kia Sorento.

Not wanting to hit the side of her new car, Beth moved the shopping cart sideways and a little closer to the protective safety of the rubber on the rear bumper.

Curt turned to unload the cart, reaching out to receive the bag she offered.

Fully Facing each other now, they were exceptionally close, as close as they had ever been. Within the span of one Mila-second, a million scenarios shot through Curt's mind.

Photographically, his eyes darted, logging every detail of her face. Her freshly moistened lips glistened, the beauty of her nose and the short, soft downy hair above the curved outline of her forehead that gently caressed her face. His glance raced to her eyes.

Without control, he felt a faint rush of sweat run over his forehead and hands. Was it the heat of the Florida sun causing this rush or was a life changing event about to unfold? Almost trace like, he stared at her.

From the depths of her wild beautiful green eyes, she invited him in. Quickly, the circles of her pupils adjusted, dilating in reaction to the instant, then becoming enlarged with anticipation.

Deep into the black centers, swirling down inside them, Curt felt himself falling into the well-like depths of her soul.

Beckoning him, they seemed to say, come closer! See what I have stored behind these mirrors of life. Come inside and see what I have saved my whole life for this special moment.

Closing his eyes, he moved ever so slightly in her direction. He smelled the freshness of her skin, her breath. He extended his hand which she took as they moved even closer towards each other. She looked into his eyes, her eyes closed. Their lips...

"EXCUSE ME!"

Shocked at the loud intrusion. Curt and Beth jumped backwards.

"Can I get by your car please? I'm sorry to bother you but I have a very important Dr.'s appointment and I just can't be late."

Looking back at each other, Curt and Beth nervously burst into laughter, then timidly, looked away.

That was close. It was Like, almost being hit by a truck or something, knowing that it was a life changing moment and yet somehow wishing it had actually happened.

It's strange when the spider of emotions begins to spin its web. You never know who will become entangled in it.

Then, her eyes came back to his as she smiled warmly. It was a partially disappointed smile. Inside, her heart longed for the moment to have been completed as she continued to look at him. Even though Curt had been injured and walked with a slight limp, she suddenly, found him nothing less than completely desirable. It had been a long time since Beth had felt the emotions that had just raced through her body.

Inside she trembled with a new sensation of life that pulsed through her. A faint twitch began in her upper right eyelid. She remembered when she was young, her eye would do that when she was under intense pressure, excited or extremely nervous. She knew that the fleeting moment was special and that it was now lost forever with no way to reclaim it.

Obviously, over the years, the dust of the digs had covered up all those wonderful feelings she carried inside. Emotions that were now completely awake. Unconsciously, she fidgeted with her shirt tail and stirred a bit with uneasiness.

He looked down at the ground then lifted his head saying half stuttering. "I'll move the truck."

Beth smiled, "Here Curt, you drive."

She flipped him the keys then turned and pushed the cart towards the return rack.

As Curt opened the door of Beth's SUV. That familiar new car smell rushed to greet him. He started the car. "Nothing like new car smell he thought to himself and that air conditioner. Man! That's the coldest air I've ever felt in an automobile. Nice Car!" He said to himself.

Perhaps, after the near miss incident that had just transpired, the cool stream of air was just what he needed.

He put the truck in gear and carefully inched forward to allow the impatient old lady the opportunity to pass.

Beth returned to the car, climbed into the passenger side and folded her legs up in the seat.

"Well, off to the races. I think we got everything we need for the cook-out." Curt smiled. " I think I'm going to need a dip in the pool after all this. Cold and refreshing."

"I know exactly what you mean. If you don't mind. Let's stop by my house on the way back and let me pick up my suit too and I'll join you."

"Certainly, Sounds good to me. I'll be glad to." Curt replied. "Let's see, you said you live just off linear park on Metro, right?"

Chapter Twelve: Homestead Calling

Rico always called in Gerald and Harold Masters when he needed something done. Truly, brothers in crime. They had a nasty reputation and would do just about anything, provided they were paid well enough to do the deed.

"Hey guys, thanks for coming by today. I've got something I need done over on Pine Island, west of Cape Coral and I thought of you two. You know where that is?"

"Yep, No problem. Harold said, no job to small, cause we do it all."

"Did you just make that up Harold? Cause if you did, it still needs some work buddy."

"Oh, it's just kind of a saying we ha..."

"Hey, let's cut through the crap." Rico charged, "Listen up."

"I want you to go see a man about a coin. Here's the phone number and the address for this guy. His name is Ohio Jim Hudson. He's a fisherman so you probably can't get ahold of him until he gets off the water, late afternoon or early evenings."

"What kind of coin is it that we are to inquire about? Anyway." "Do you want us to steal it?"

"It's an old gold coin and it's valuable. I want you to try to negotiate a deal for it. Tell him the deal is a cash deal, no questions asked. Also, ask him if he knows if there are any more available."

"How much should we offer him? Do you have an idea of how much you are willing to give for it?"

"Yes, I do. I'm willing to start the offer at $50,000. If you get ahold of him by phone, tell him you will deliver cash on your next meeting in exchange for the coin."

"$50,000! Son of a Bitch Rico! That must be some coin."

"It is Harold. I want this done on the QT as quickly as possible. I'm willing to pay 10% of the coin offer to do the job. You in?"

"Dam Skippy sounds like a deal to me. You in Gerald? GERALD!"

"Yeah, Yeah Sure H., whatever you say. I'm in."

"Ok, guys, be on your way and get back to me as soon as you can and by the way, use the back door when you leave gentlemen."

"Sure Rico, no problem."

Herold and Gerald left and headed for their office. It was an office of a different kind. A shop was more like it, complete with hand drills, a chop saw, a torch, welder, tools and two steel benches.

An overhead door provided access from the rear. Located near a Hispanic neighborhood on the south-east side of Miami. There was no window on the blacked out-front door. Inside a small desk up was situated front with a phone on it. They found that this set up worked well for them as on numerous occasions, when specialized work was required, or to complete certain unusual jobs.

There was an oversized reinforced steel chair in the only other room, next to the toilet. A length of Rope hung from the chair arm; blood stains could still be seen nearby on the floor. Like they said. They would do just about anything if they were paid enough.

"So, what do you think H. should we make a trip over to see this guy or shall we call him first?"

"Let's give him a call, like Rico said, to get the ball rolling. If we make the deal, then we can get the cash from Rico and get this done all in one trip."

"Sounds good to me. What's his number?"

"It's right here. Let me dial it."

Harold called the number up until around 7:30 that night but, no one answered. "This must not be a cell phone number cause there's no way to leave a message. I'll bet this is his home phone."

"One more call Gerald, then we use another approach."

"They waited till 8:45 then called the number again."

"Hello!"

"Hello, is this Jim Hudson. Ohio Jim Hudson?"

"Yes, it's me. Whatcha need?"

"Mr. Hudson, this is Harold Masters over in Homestead, Florida. How are you this evening?"

"I'm good, but it's been a long day."

"Mr. Hudson. We represent a client on the Florida East coast and, well, we've heard it through the grapevine that you have an old gold coin that might be for sale. Our client wishes to purchase the coin if you're willing to negotiate on it."

"Fella, I have no idea what you're talking about. Gold coin. I've never even seen a gold coin much less have one for sale."

"Seriously Mr. Hudson, we have it on pretty good authority that you have an old coin or artifact as it was called and that it may be for sale."

"Ok, well, let's say I did have a coin like the one you're talking about. How much would the offer be."

"Our Client is willing to offer you $50,000 dollars cash."

"$50,000, Shit, it's worth a lot more than that."

"Mr. Hudson, would you be willing to meet and negotiate a deal. Remember, it will be a cash deal with no questions asked."

"I don't know, give me a few days to think about it. I not sure about it besides, I don't even know you."

"Alright Mr Hudson, If that's the way you're going to play it. We'll be in touch and the phone went silent."

"Be in Touch! That sounded a little rough. This guy sounds like a wise guy or something."

Jim hung up the phone. "This is moving way too fast," he said out loud. "I gotta think about it a little bit."

Jim stood up, then made his way into the kitchen where he pulled a bottle of Crown Royal off the shelf. From the overhead freezer above the fridge, he grabbed some ice and filled the glass. He poured 4 inches of whiskey over the ice.

After, shaking the highball glass a couple of times for chill, he tilted his head back and drank the entire thing in one continuous gulping swallow. Then sat the glass down on the kitchen cabinet.

"Dam Jennis, I needed that one."

Not knowing what to think, his mind began to run wild, flittering in different directions. Who was it that had called him? How did he know about the coin and How the fuck did the guy get my phone number?

"I've got a mullet trip tomorrow but, after that, I'll have to talk to Beth about this. I'm positive she didn't give me up."

The tone of the phone call wasn't good. It worried him to the point he thought that he could possibly be in danger because of his non-co-operation with the man on the other end. The guy sounded like he meant business. He had no idea what the guy meant when he said, we'll be in touch.

That night, before Jim went to bed, he pulled out a pad and pen to jot Beth a quick note. Obviously, he didn't have a good feeling about the call.

"Beth: I got a call from a guy tonight that wanted to buy the coin. I have no idea how he found out about it, much less, how he got my phone number."

"I still trust you but, somehow this has got out and I've got a real uneasy feeling about it all."

"I believe the old sayings are true about gold. Trouble follows it."

"Here's hoping we are able to discuss this letter together again but, should something happen, I leave you with something to think about."

"I lied about where I found the coin. I did it to throw anyone off that might wish to interfere before I found out what it was all about. Looks like my fears may be realized."

"Beth, remember this:"

"What we held is hidden with the dollars at home."

"A tiny key will unlock the treasure."

"I miss my DARLING Jennis."

"Think it all through. Then you should know what I know. Sorry I mislead you."

"Hope to see you again soon."

Best, Ohio Jim

Jim tore the note off the steno pad, folded it up and put it in an envelope he addressed to Beth at the College. Just for insurance, he would drop it in the Bokeelia mailbox on his way to the dock the next morning.

Feeling like the weight of the day had set upon his eyelids, he laid down and closed his eyes to rest.

Chapter Thirteen: Poolside

Just as Curt and Beth pulled back into the drive at Curt's house, Beth's cell phone rang. Beth looked at the phone and said excitedly, "It's Jolene. I want to take this. OK?"

"Sure!"

"Hello, Jolene, how are you today?"

"I'm just fine, what are you up to?"

"Well, actually I'm going to a cookout at Curt's house. He's the guy I told you about. The guy I met at Starbucks."

"Ah Ha," Jolene exclaimed. "You mean that handsome, teddy bear, Pilot Dude. Right?"

"Yep, that's the one."

"So, what's up with you today?" Beth asked

"Oh, they cancelled practice today. The field got flooded when a guy mowing the field broke a pipe in the sprinkler system. So, I was calling to see if you wanted to swing by the Boat House for some lunch with me."

"Ah, can you hold on for one second Jolene?"

Sure.

Beth held her phone against her leg to muffle the sound and said; "Curt, didn't you tell me that some of your buddies were coming over too? Are they all bringing dates?"

"Three guys are coming to be exact and only one is bringing a date." Curt said.

"Awesome, this is Jolene on the phone, can we ask her to come join the party?"

"Absolutely, Curt said with a big smile. Ask her to get right on over here."

"OK, let me see if she can come."

"Jolene, Curt is having a Football, BBQ, pool party this afternoon. Some of his buddies are going to be here and two are single. Can you make it? We'd love to have you."

"Beth, I'd love to. That's the reason I called you. They cancelled practice leaving me with nothing to do today. I don't know them but since you'll be there, I can't think of a reason I shouldn't. It sounds like a good time."

"Too much fun she said. It'll be a blast."

Beth gave Jolene Curt's address and told her: "Don't forget your swimsuit. His pool is beautiful."

"OK, you know me, it won't take me long to get ready. I'll gather up my things and be there in an hour or so. See you shortly. Thanks, Bye, Bye".

Beth clicked the button to end the call.

"Thank You so much Curt, that is so nice of you to let Jolene to come over."

"There's always room for another pretty face at a party. Isn't there? Jerry and Brian will be excited for sure. Maybe even grateful," Curt smiled. "They're both single."

"I hope they're sports buffs because Jolene is a walking sports encyclopedia."

"Yep, glad you asked for her to come over Beth. The guys will be excited to meet her too and who knows what will happen. I know for a fact that Brian is a bigtime sports fanatic himself."

"Awesome. Would you like for me to put the beer in that igloo chest and dump the ice over it?"

"Sure, if you'd like too."

"Curt. Didn't you say another couple was coming also?"

"I did indeed, Michael and Mary will be here for sure. They've been together for as long as I've known them. They're great people. He runs a local Air Conditioning business and she's an RN. You'll like them, I know. Especially Mary she's a sweetheart."

"Awesome" Beth replied. "I can't wait to meet them".

Beth helped Curt set out two folding tables and placed plastic table-cloths, one on each. Together, they brought out a huge stack of steaming ribs, sauce, potato salad, chips and the rest of the party food. Beth placed it tastefully next to the plates, forks and spoons.

"Curt, I love your Miami Dolphin Solo Cups."

"Thanks Beth. Check out the napkins."

"Curt really! Miami Dolphin napkins too?"

Sheepishly, he mustered up a big smile. Curt loved the Miami Dolphins and he liked to tend bar for his friends so, you didn't have to look far to find him when the big game was on.

Curt had the bar built as the center attraction of his spacious poolside lanai. Above and behind it was a 72" flat screen TV. Tropical themed neon beer signs were on the wall, either side of the big screen. This place was beautiful and as good if not better than any sports bar in town with viewing access of the game anywhere a person chooses to set inside the enclosure.

For convenience, there was outside access to an inside bathroom from the pool area too. Curt always said he thought it kept his pool a lot more sanitary, in addition to providing a place for his guests to change into their swimsuits. It really made it nice.

It wasn't long until Jolene arrived at Curt's house. In typical fashion, high pitch screams and laughter were omitted freely by the duo while completing the reunion.

Jerry and Brian soon arrived too. Curt introduced them to Jolene and Beth.

"This one's mine", Curt said, while holding his hand above Beth's head, "So don't get any ideas."

Everyone found their way into the game area of the lanai and made themselves comfortable.

Addressing his guests, Curt orated loud enough for all to hear. "The game's coming on in 15 minutes so if you want to eat you'd better get yourself and plate and get with the program cause once it starts, I'm glued to the TV. Beer is in the coolers, iced tea is in the crock and please throw all your trash in that big can over there when you're done. Thanks everyone for coming. It's going to be a great day."

Jolene and Brian were immediately attracted to each other. Both were avid sports buffs and seemed to have a lot in common.

They talked so much, it sounded like two sports announcers' competing for the microphone. Neither one running out of sports stories or stats. Jerry sipped his cold beer, relaxed and enjoyed the game from the comfort of a big recliner lounger.

Curt was ecstatic when Miami won the game. The lions never got it together. Those are the kind of games a fan loves too. Like Oklahoma Coach, Barry Switzer used to always say; Let's Hang a half a hundred on the opposition before halftime then, coast for to a victory. Afterward the game, they all chose up sides and played a round of water volleyball. The afternoon passed quickly.

Brian and Jolene left for Duffy's sports bar together to catch another game.

"Well, they're all gone now. What a wonderful day. I had such a great time Curt and the food was marvelous."

A clap of thunder came thru gray clouds that had moved into the area. Light rain started to fall so Beth and Curt moved back inside.

Beth, would you care for anything else. I'm going to fix me a kick-back cocktail now that everyone is gone. I think I've earned a little time for myself."

"Sure, I'll have one, but make it real light though."

"Absolutely dear. As you wish. Vodka Rocks for you Beth?"

Beth looked shocked. "Not hardly."

"Just kidding." Curt said smiling back at her.

"I'd like a light rum and tonic, no lime please, lots of ice."

"Coming up."

Curt fixed their drinks and returned to where Beth was sitting in the lanai.

"It's a beautiful evening." Beth sighed.

"It certainly is. There's nothing like a night in Florida when a little shower comes to cool things down. I've sat here under the eve of this lanai on many an evening. It's quite enjoyable."

As Curt stares into the mist of the rain, he comments;
"The canal behind the house breathes deeply with every tide, moving constantly, yet it goes nowhere.
Ravenous in appetite, every drop of falling water is welcomed, then quietly consumed.
It's a lonely watery road that affords travel to only the few with means."

"Youthfully, each drop of rain recklessly announces its presence, as liquid rings radiate from shock of the union. Then... all individuality ceases."

"Such is life as a comparison. One who makes decisions in haste, to make a commitment out of loneliness is often denied what the future holds in store for them. Becoming part of a group that never finds fulfillment."

"Very profound Curt."

"I like it. I didn't know you were a philosopher too."

"Not so much." He said. "Just thinking out loud more than anything else. I've enjoyed spending the day with you Beth. Ah, and the others too, of course but your being here made it exceptionally nice."

"Likewise, Curt. I have to admit those ribs you cooked were stellar. Very good!"

"You know? About this afternoon, at the grocery store, I don't know what got into me. I hope you don't think me too forward, I..."

"No, No not at all. By the way, I'd like to compliment you. You've done a nice job here. Your home is not only beautiful but it's very comfortable too, I like it. You know, come to think of it, you never did show me the rest of the house."

"Well, the bedrooms are all that's left and I..."

"Curt looked up to see Beth tilt her head with a slightly raised eyebrow."

"Blushing for no reason other than surprise", Curt asked.

"Beth. Would you like to see the rest of the house?"

Beth sat her drink down on the table, stood up and offered her hand to him.

Then replied. "I thought you'd never ask."

Chapter Fourteen: The Mullet Were Thick

Jim had worked hard with the striped mullet crew. Casting all day long with a net that weighs 35 pounds and opens to 24' is tough on an old man. This year there were tons more mullet than last year.

It was very profitable for all on board today, they all agreed. Some would be smoked, some pickled, some would be made into mullet butter and some would be frozen to sell as bait.

Commercial buyers waited anxiously at the county dock. Talking amongst themselves, the air was thick with smoke from their cigars and the smell of fish stored on the dock. Each man hoping to get the jump the other buyer in order to make a good mullet purchase.

Mullet season always brings allot of money into the Pine Island area. Over and above normal mullet trade, seems like there was a honey and smoked mullet vendor on every prime high traffic corner in the island area.

With their pick-ups parked in backwards, Jars of honey were displayed on box tops in the beds. Iced smoked mullet filled four or five igloo ice chests beside them. Sometimes they sold large freshly caught shrimp too, whatever would make a buck.

Today, back at the dock, Jim helped unload the ships hold. Afterwards he stopped by the pay window to pick up his share of the days catch, then headed towards his truck.

The day had passed quickly. Seems his mind was more on what had taken place lately, Beth, the coin and the unusual phone call rather than how tough the back-breaking work was.

"I still got it", Jim thought, as he slowly climbed into his truck. I can still run with the big dogs. Stretching a bit, his back and shoulders were sore. His legs a bit shaky somewhat succumbing to the strenuous day of labor throwing the nets. "I'm not getting any younger though. An ice-cold beer is what I'm thinking. Maybe two. Think I'll stop in Captain Con's Bar before I head home."

"I've earned this one."

North on Stringfellow, Jim drove right on past the road he lived on his way to Captain Con's Restaurant / Bar at the end of the island. "Gotta eat too and I sure as hell don't feel like cookin tonight."

Jim walked in and took his usual stool at the bar. Jill, the bartender, didn't even ask she just took out his favorite brew and poured it into an ice-cold glass. This was an exercise that they had practiced many times before, on different occasions. Mostly predictable without much demand. Jim's demeanor was usually easy going.

He slammed down a couple of beers while he consumed a large bowl of seafood chowder filled with small, salty oyster crackers.

"Dammit, that's some good shit right there," he thought.

"One more brewsky before the road please."

Jill! Anticipating his request, she was already pouring another beer for him when he asked.

"Workin for a bigger tip are Ya?"

Jill smiled and placed the frosty mug on a new bar napkin in front of him.

Jim held the ice-cold mug handle between two fingers and his thumb. The heat of his fingers left a print through the frost down to the glass on the side of the handle.

"You know, every time I come here, I end up thinking the same thing."

He stared at the side of the iced mug.

"Look at this Jill. See the bubbles that appear out of nowhere, then causally rise to the top,

Like they're escaping from captivity, then for no reason they suddenly pop!"

"Strange, don't you think?"

They both turned to smile at each other.

"That's just what beer does, she said, guess that's part of what makes it taste so good."

It is pretty to watch too.

"Better to drink than watch," Jim roared. "I made a rhyme too!"

"What'r the damages?"

$15. 75 should do it Jim, tax included."

"Jim laid a twenty down on the bar. See you next time sweetie. Thanks, a lot."

Jim pushed through the wooden screen door exit and made his way towards his truck. Heavy dew had settled on the windshield. He hadn't got around to buying new wipers for the truck yet, but it wasn't far to his house from where he was.

"I'll be OK," he thought.

Driving home from Con's was like an old habit. He had done it so many times it was like the truck was on auto pilot.

Jim pulled up in front of the house, walked up to the door, turned the key and opened it. He flipped the lights on once the door opened.

"Son of a Bitch! Who the fuck are you? How'd you get in fucking my house anyway."

Two men were sitting quietly in Jim's living room. Each wearing old style felt brimmed hat and light overcoats.

"Mr. Hudson? Ohio Jim Hudson?"

Jim yelled at the two men with all his muster, "You Mother Fuckers have no right to break into my house." Jim looked for something to defend himself with, but the closest thing was the bottle of crown royal. Not even a good handle on that bottle.

"Now, now calm down," Mr. Hudson. "I talked to you last night, we want to make you and offer for the gold coin."

"Coin, I told you I need time to think about it!"

"We've got a lot of cash with us and I hate to go back to Miami empty handed." "Why don't you just calm down a little bit and let's talk about this deal."

"Deal, there is no deal, I told you I needed time to think about it."

"Mr. Hudson, I have in this bag, $50,000 dollars cash that we are offering you for the coin."

"$50,000, Bullshit, it's worth at least $80,000 any day of the week, I've been told."

"You were told? Mr. Hudson. By Whom? Does someone else know about the coin in question?"

"None of your fucking business, I looked it up on the internet and things like the one I have go for a hell of a lot more than no dam $50,000 dollars."

"Do you have the coin with you here? I know, how about you show us the coin and we'll up the offer by adding another $15,000, say, let's make it an even $65,000 cash."

So far, Gerald had sat next to H. as patiently as his attention span would allow. Looking down, he shuffled his feet on the throw rug trying to remove a small rack of sandburs from the sole of his shoe. Muttering to himself; "I hate those fucking sandburs."

H turned to Gerald and said. "What the fuck are you talking about? Can't you see I'm talking to the man here about this deal?"

"Oh, sorry H."

"H turned back to Jim. Would you take $65,000 money cash for the coin?"

As Jim started to speak, Fidgeting, Gerald stood up and moved around a bit. With his hand under his overcoat he turned towards the conversation.

"I told you, It's worth at least $80,000. Besides..."

Thuu Thuu Thuu. Smoke escaped through a large hole in the front of Gerald's overcoat. Gerald just grinned.

Ohio Jim reeled from the impact of the silenced bullets hitting him in the chest. He staggered backwards and fell...

"Gerald, No! What the fuck have you done, you idiot!"

"Well, he was being too hard to deal with and I guess I just lost it."

"Dammit, I was doing the negotiating and we didn't even get the coin. Now we don't even know where it is. We got no information and you fucking shoot the guy before we get the deal done. You stupid bastard!"

Looking upwards through glazed eyes, reaching out his hand as if to connect to something. "JENNIS," Jim cried out,

Blood ran from Ohio Jim's nose and mouth as he said, "Jennis", once again. Slowly his hand dropped as his eyes moved into a blackened distant stare. Ohio Jim Hudson was dead.

"What the fuck is wrong with you man? You fucking shoot the guy right in the middle of me talking to him."

"Jennis! What the fuck does Jennis mean. Dammit? Is that a town and place? What the fuck?"

"Dammit Gerald, what does Jennis mean?"

"I have no idea H."

"Shut up you stupid bastard. If you weren't my brother, I'd fucking shoot you myself." "Rico is going to be one pissed off Son of a Bitch."

"Do we have to tell him H?"

"Do we have to tell him? The guy is dead. We've got $65,000 of Rico's money and no coin. Hell, yes, we have to tell him. Now we got to give all the money back too. Shit, I'm not looking forward to that either."

"Do you think we ought to look around for the coin H?"

"I suppose so. I don't have a fucking clue where to start. Looks like a pauper lives here."

"Put your fucking gloves on and go look in the bedroom. I'll look around in here."

"Look slowly and be careful not to leave anything that could connect us to this scene. Don't get carried away opening up drawers and don't step in that blood. Be fucking careful man. This is already so fucked up."

"I'm sorry H."

"Shut the fuck up and do what I tell you."

H. walked to the sill over the hearth of the old fireplace in the living room. A picture of a woman in an old frame sat there partially covered in dust. Next to the picture was a round rattan reed platter full of shells and a few sand dollars. Next to it, an old broken pipe was all there was to see.

"Gerald. Find anything?"

"Nothing, this guy doesn't own shit. There's nothing to even look through."

"Let's get the fuck out-a-here."

Gerald and H left the house holding onto the screen door, so it wouldn't slam. Walking back down the lane to the tree grove where they had hidden the car H said. "Shit, we're not going to make a fucking dime off this gig either." H started the car and drove for at least a half block before he turned the headlights on.

Back on the highway, on the way over, once they were east of the Marco Island turnoff on I-75, H. keyed up his cell phone to pick up a tower and dialed.

"Rico, Hello Rico, H here. I'm afraid I've got some bad news. That Jim guy is dead."

"Did you get the coin?"

"No, we didn't get anything. Not even any information that would lead us to it."

Well, good fucking deal man. What the hell happened? You've still got my money right.

"Oh, yeah, I got the money in the bag."

"Well, in the middle of negotiating the deal, right when I was taking to the guy, Gerald ups and shoots the guy."

"One shot killed him? Sometimes one shot can make a man talk."

"Well, not exactly, he busted off three rounds.

There is one thing Rico. Before he died, he lifted up one hand like he was reaching for someone, then, he sputtered the word Jennis."

"Jennis, what the hell does that mean? What the hell is wrong with your brother H? What the Fuck?"

"Ok, Shit happens. Look. You know the big public restroom at the south end of Miami along the beach walk? The one where the bicycle rental is located."

"Yes, I know where that is."

"Meet me there 11:30 tonight. It's usually mostly deserted by then and bring my money."

"Ok Rico. See you there. Sorry man."

It was getting close to 11:30. Rico parked two blocks away from the rendezvous site with H and Gerald. He walked causally in the direction of the building, scanning the area, paying special attention, looking around for anyone that may see him that could botch his plans.

Rico walked completely around the building, clearing the area before he entered.

"H. I'm upset with you guys. This meant a whole lot to me. Now it's totally botched. Did you check all the shitter stalls when you got here?"

"We Checked'em, the place is empty. I'm sorry Rico, we won't make a dime on it either. We know the rules. "Only Performance Pays."

"Gerald, did you use a silencer, so no one heard anything?"

Yes Sir, it's my signature trademark.

The only fucking thing signature about you Gerald is your fucking stupidity. You have no idea what this has cost me."

"Do you still have the gun you used to ace the guy?"

"I do, I've got it right here."

"H, is that the money?"

"Yes, Sir. All $65,000 of it."

"OK, Great. Gerald, let me see the gun you used. Are there any bullets left in it?"

Gerald replies; "Dam Skippy. Eight in the mag and one in the chamber."

As Rico inspected the gun, he slid the safety off the Beretta 40. Thuu Thuu Thuu, the gun rocked in Rico's hand as Gerald grabbed at his chest. Falling to his knees, Rico pointed the gun to Gerald's forehead and pulled the trigger again. "That's for being stupid and stupid ends here."

"H, sorry about that but you know the rules. Loose cannons shoot holes in their own boat. This idiot had to go. On second thought, I think I probably need some protection in case you decide you want revenge"; Before H could act, Rico turned quickly and fired three times hitting him squarely thru the heart and lungs.

"You know how I hate loose ends." Rico said.

Aiming at H's forehead, Rico pulled the trigger once more just for insurance. H dropped to the floor like a sack of mackerel falling from a two-story building.

Rico immediately wiped the gun handle down then laid it in H's hand, forcing H's hand around the grips. Rico pulled the trigger so that the gun fired again hitting the wall. After all, Rico knew there had to be GSR on one of them in order to sell the deal.

Being careful not to step in the blood, Rico picked up the money bag and flipped the lights off as he quietly exited the building.

In a roundabout direction, Rico made his way back to his car. He remembered what his old man had always taught him about the 6 P's. Proper Planning Prevents Piss Poor Performance.

By parking blocks away, his car wouldn't be seen anywhere even close to where the two brother's bodies would be discovered.

As he walked in the darkness towards his car, a rush came over him. "Such power he thought", as he laughed aloud.

"Gerald had to go but the rush came when I shot H. Like an instant replay with such a powerful, pleasing result. Why was the moment so fulfilling, almost sexual, so exhilarating? "Amazing", he thought. "Simply amazing."

Well, now I've got to start over. If I'm going to have any chance at finding that treasure. I need information. Information that, so far, I've been denied, by idiots. I wonder if that woman professor at FSW knows anything? Guess we'll have to see what tomorrow brings..."

Chapter Fifteen: What About Jim

"Hello Curt. Can you meet me in the Ace parking lot next to Winn Dixie on the Parkway? I've been trying to get in touch with of Ohio Jim for the last two days. I tried him all last night up until 11:30 and yesterday starting at 6:00 AM. No one answers. I want to go out to his house and see if something's wrong. Will you go with me?"

"Sure Hon. Why don't you just come by my house and we'll leave from here."

"Ok Great. Thanks so much. I don't like the feelings I'm having. Beth went by Curt's house to pick him up."

When she arrived, Curt walked out to the car to greet her.

"Curt. You have a gun, don't you? Didn't you say you still had the one you use to carry when you were in the service?"

"I do indeed Beth. I've still got it."

"Well, for no reason other than I'd feel allot better about it, would you please bring it with you when you come? I don't know why. Just in case I guess."

"Sure, give me just a second. I'll run back in and get it. Are we going to need bullets too?" Curt said with a grin.

"Oh Curt, don't be such a joker. This is serious."

"Ok, I was just trying to make a funny, maybe get you out of such a serious mood."

"I love you to pieces but not now please Curt."

Down Veteran's Parkway then across the Matlacha draw bridge they went, then on to Center Junction on Pine Island. "Now turn right on Stringfellow the GPS says and we go almost clear to the end of the island, then make a left on Barrancas Rd. His house should be the last one on the left, 5720 Judge Bean Rd. Turn left

114

here, on Barrancas rd., now right two blocks to Judge Bean Rd and follow it around clear to the western end."

"Curt look at all that police tape across the front door and that's his truck. I knew it. Something has happened. Don't guess we'll need the gun after all." Beth said.

"There's no one around, do you think we can look inside?"
"I don't know why not."

Curt pulled open the screen door, reached in and twisted the doorknob. As the door opened the police tape broke as it swung open.
"Hold it Beth, it doesn't look good.
There's a big blood stain on the floor and from the tracks, it looks like someone was removed here by on a wheeled gurney or something."
Curt pointed. "Are you sure you want to go in there?"

"NO, NO! Are you saying some one was killed here?"

"I'd say that from the amount of blood on the floor someone was either severely injured or killed. Since its Ohio Jim's house and you haven't been able to reach him, I'd say there's pretty good odds that Jim was the one involved."
"You're probably right. I hope not but, that is a lot of blood on the floor. Curt, we'll have to find out. But for now, I want to take a quick look around. I don't want to seem cold hearted or uncaring, but we may never be able to get a chance to get back here."
"There's actually not much here. Hardly even any furniture."

Beth scanned the room, then walked over to the hearth of the fireplace on the end wall. Doesn't look like this old fireplace has been used in years. It's so dusty!"

"This must be Jennis." Beth said, as she looked at the picture of the lady contained in the old frame.

"Nice smile," Beth thought.

"Who's Jennis?" Curt asked

"His wife. He told me she was killed in hurricane Charlie back in 2004. He's been alone ever since."

"Curt. Look here. That's was one of the clues in his note to me. I love my DARLING Jennis. Don't you think it strange that the word Darling was all in caps. It must mean something, but it makes no sense to me right now."

She looked further. "The only things left up here are this old broken smoking pipe and here's a fiber tray of shells and some sand dollars."

"Sand dollars? Maybe he was saving them for a rainy day." Curt retorted.

"Curt, look here again in the note; Ohio Jim said, "What we held is hidden with the dollars at home". Could it be that simple? Could he have meant sand dollars?"

"Oh My God, Look! Here it is. Here's the coin under the sand dollars. See the markings. He must have covered it in egg and floor see. He covered it in flour, so it would resemble a sand dollar in color and hid it in plain sight. No one would ever have thought to look for it there."

She lifted it from the tray and put it in her coat pocket.

"Amazing." Curt replied.

"We better get out of here before someone comes. Let's go now and try to find out what if anything has happened to Jim. I hope he's OK but like I said. I don't have a good feeling about any of this."

Beth grabbed her water bottle off the hearth on the way out. They pulled the door shut and re-attached the tape across the door.

As they drove away, retracing their path away from Ohio Jim's house, Curt, noticed a guy mowing his yard down the street. Beth, slow down and pull over here so I can talk to that guy. "Excuse me. Do you know anything about what happened at the house at the end of the street?"

The guy stopped the mower and walked over towards Beth's car. "The guy that lived there was found shot to death. Yep, we heard he was shot three times. God love him. Ohio Jim Hudson was his name. I knew him. No one knows who did it but, I guess it happened night before last. Why, did you know him?"

"Ah, no, not actually, my girlfriend was a friend of his. She couldn't get ahold of him, so we just came out to see if anything was wrong. I guess being shot to death is plenty enough to have had gone wrong."

"I here tell that Jill, the bartender at Captain Con's bar, was the last one to have seen him alive. Too bad too, he was a really nice guy. All he ever did was work and talk about his wife that the hurricane stole from him. Guess he's with her now."

"Ok, Man, sad to hear about it. Thanks, so much for the information." Curt said. "We better be getting along now, thanks again."

Curt rolled up the window as Beth drove on.

On the way back to Curt's house they talked. "There's a lot more to this than we know. Beth, you're going to have to be careful.

117

Someone may connect you to all this. It obvious that they're playing for keeps."

"It's horrible Curt. Ohio Jim shot to death. Do you think it was over the coin? How would anyone else know about it? Jim told me that I was the only one he had said anything to about it. Well remember in the note he made reference to a phone call that upset him. That's why he sent you the note that contained the clues. You've solved one of the clues already. Now, all we have to do is solve the others."

"Let's head on back to the house and have a drink just to calm down with. Truthfully Beth, I really wish you would consider staying at my house tonight. I don't want for you to suffer a similar fate as Ohio Jim did."

"Well, I guess not!"

"All I mean is, I can protect you a lot better on my home turf with the weapons I have at hand perhaps allot better than you could by yourself at your place. If they thought you knew anything, whomever found Ohio Jim may be looking for you too. I don't know but I'm not willing to risk it."

"Absolutely", Beth replied.

Curt looked at Beth. "Tonight, is going to be one of those rare occasions when I sleep with that gun fully loaded real close to my pillow. Know what I mean."

Beth mustered a slight smile and sighed.

"Thanks Curt. I'll feel allot safer with you tonight..."

Chapter Sixteen: Jolene Came By

Next day, after softball practice, Jolene stopped by Beth's office to check in on her.

"You feeling any better girlfriend?"

"Not really Jolene."

"That's a shame about your friend Ohio Jim. Getting shot three times point blank is pretty heavy I have to admit. I'm no expert but It sounds like a hit to me. But, like you say, who would want to kill him."

"Beth, could there be anyone else that knew he came to see you about that coin?"

"Not that I know of Jolene. I can't think of a single sole who...No, now wait just a minute. I never thought about until you provoked the thought. That dam Dr. Alvera overheard the whole conversation between Ohio Jim and me. That smelly SOB is just slimy enough to have told someone hoping to get in on the deal if anything turned up. I have no idea who to talk to about it though. If I go to the police, they might think I am involved, and I can't take a chance on that. I'll tell Curt and ask him what he thinks about it."

"I plan on staying at Curt's house again tonight. I feel safe there amongst the other fringe benefits of sharing his company."

They both smiled at each other.

"Good stuff huh!"

"Really Good Stuff!" Beth announced emphatically.

"Are you about ready to leave yet? I'm parked in the lot outside by your car. I'll walk out with you."

"Sounds good. It's getting late and I'm really tired. This has been an extremely stressful day with all the goings on. I can't wait to get back over to Curt's to just kick back and relax a little bit."

Beth gathered up her satchel and picked up a book that she planned to continue reading later that evening.

"Let me just lock my office door and we'll be off."

As the girls walked outside the office building, the streetlights came on, partially lighting the surrounding campus. They headed on towards the parking lot where Jolene had parked parallel to Beth's car.

Crossing the wider handicap parking spaces near their cars they were shocked by the sound of loud tire screeching as a black cargo van headed straight towards them. The van slammed on its brakes and slid a bit sideways blocking the girl's path to their cars. Three men dressed in black with black ski masks jumped out of the side door of the van and ran towards Beth and Jolene. Two of the men grabbed Beth. Screaming, Beth kicked and clawed at her assailants. Together the two men overpowered her. One man held her arms tightly behind her back while the other quickly slapped a strap of gray duct tape over her mouth.

Beth gasped. She was barely able to breath much less escape.

The other man clasp Jolene by the waist, lifted her off the ground and threw her into the side door of the van. Instinctively, like rough housing with her older brothers back home, she yanked away as they both fell outside of the truck. Jolene swirled around and hit him with all her might, smashing her elbow straight into the nose of her foe.

Crack was the sound as blood shot forth from the ski mask. Instantly, he let go of her.

"You broke my fucking nose bitch!"

Jolene ran towards Beth. But her attempt at Beth's rescue was too late. The other men had already tossed her, headfirst, into the van.

Holding his bleeding nose, he turned around, "I'm gonna kill..."

"Get in the fucking truck man. NOW! we got no time for this." The man that attacked Jolene ran for the truck, leaping into the side door just as it raced out of the parking lot.

It was just dark enough that Jolene couldn't get any sort of read on the tag number of the van.

Jolene was never one for crying. She was much too tough for that, but right now, shocked and overwhelmed, she couldn't help herself. Sobbing, she walked around the parking lot, picked up her purse and gathered the things that had scattered about and what she could find of Beth's too. No phone. "Where's my phone?"

Her phone was nowhere to be found.

"I've got to get to Curt's house now," she thought. "They've got Beth. He'll know what to do. I just know it."

Speeding away, the driver of the van ordered for one of the men to find Beth's cell phone and toss it out of the window. A phone with a GPS location button turned on could lead the police or whomever straight to their hideout.

"I've got it right here."

"Toss the dam thing." The driver commanded.

The man behind the passenger seat, hung his arm out of the window. With all his might, he threw the phone down at the concrete from the moving van as hard as he could. Upon impact the glass face of the phone shattered. The outside plastic shell, motherboard and batteries of the phone all scattered like a broken sack of marbles.

Confident that the threat was eliminated; "I doubt that fucking phone will lead anyone to us. Shit, I bet there aint two pieces left of it any bigger than a dam chigger, he roared in a shrieking, off tone laugh. Nice work when you can get it men."

Screaming, Beth kicked and struggled to free herself.

Tape her wrists. I don't want her getting loose.

Beth continued to struggle as she screamed through the tape covering her mouth.

"Pinch her nose shut. That'll shut the bitch up. When she can't breathe, she'll quit the dramatics."

"Get a blindfold on her too and go through her purse. See what's in it and make sure nothing falls out. Anything could be a clue to what's needed, and we may learn something from what's inside it. Women have a habit of keeping too much in their purse for their own good anyway."

The van sped back towards the Caloosahatchee, Big River Bridge onto the exit ramp marked McGregor Street, then disappeared in the shadows of the lightless streets of lower westside Ft Myers gang town.

Jolene gathered everything she could see from the parking lot while trying to pull herself together. Twisting the key, she started her car, slammed it into gear and headed towards Curt's house. Onward across the bridge then thru the neighborhood, racing towards his driveway, her car slid sideways and crashed into Curt's neighbor's concrete mailbox on arrival. The noise had no more settled when Curt appeared from behind his car in his driveway.

"Dammit, my car." Jolene said.

"Jolene, what's going on?"

Jolene burst into tears crying out to Curt. They got her, they got her. Some men kidnapped Beth."

"Who? Who got her?"

Curt wanted to think that this just wasn't happening but, from the mailbox crash to Jolene's hysterical state, he knew this was definitely for real.

"Jolene, what happened? Where is Beth? Sweetheart snap out of it Jolene. "When did this happen?"

"They just now took her, some guys dressed in black, probably not more than 15 minutes ago. They got us in the parking lot at FSW."

"Dammit." Curt said. "Why"

Curt looked down at the floor. For the first time in years he felt shaky, inadequate and helpless. No, he realized that what he felt inside was pure fear. Exactly what he felt when he was shot down during Desert Shield. Incapacitated, trapped inside the chopper wreckage, paralyzed without the ability to move, he found himself praying that the allies or his own men found him before the enemy did. Knowing, full well, what his fate would be, if the enemy made his position first.

The news that Beth had been kidnapped was like a knife though his chest, he was wounded just as badly, if not more so, than the wounds he had suffered in the crash.

Fear wears an ugly face when a person is forced to stare back at it, eye to eye, who will blink first? Confidence was what he needed to fuel this fight but where could he find it? It was indeed fear now that struck though his heart. Fear for Beth, for her safety, her very existence. He closed his eyes to picture the curvature of her face. It was at that moment he realized where his fear originated from. It was coming from inside of him. It was coming straight from his heart. It was the helplessness of the position he now found himself in. It was fear for the woman that, Yes, Curt suddenly realized, he feared for the woman that he had fallen in love with. "I'm in love with her," he said to himself. "Oh My God," he said aloud.

To find love is to find life and exhilaration. To lose Love can be much worse than death.

Love, the greatest emotion on earth demands it be held sacred and protected down deep inside and that was exactly where Curt felt the pain coming from. Way down deep inside.

It seemed like such a long time since Curt had talked to God but for some reason this very moment seemed like the perfect time to re-establish contact with him.

Looking up as if to see him in the clouds above, Curt spoke out with a loud pleading voice.

"Dear God in Heaven; In the name of Jesus, keep Beth safe from harm. Encircle your army of angels around her with their shields up, their swords drawn to fight off all evil and keep her safe, lest she dash her foot upon a stone. Protect her Awesome Lord. Amen!"

"Jolene, we have to do something. Did you call the police?"

"No, no I didn't. I guarantee you though, the local police where I come from couldn't find their asses with four hands and a new Victor flashlight. Do you think it's even worth a call?"

"Well, Good or incompetent, we have to have some help. These next few hours are crucial, and I understand that these Lee County authorities are pretty good at what they do. Regardless, we've got to find a way to get Beth back and they may have some ideas."

Chapter Seventeen: Rico's Quest

Darkness reluctantly released its grip on the eastern sky as the sun rose to claim its victory over the night. As a Phoenix rising from the sea, lighting the eastern sky announcing the beginning of another day. Offering each person in the city of neon another chance to finish what they had not been able to accomplish the day before.

Early each morning, the big hotels and high-rise buildings cast elongated shadows that creep down the streets and into the alleyways in an attempt to cover up what had taken place there in the darkness just hours before. Then, greedily gathered together, grew short and withdrew to wait for another chance to come forth on the morrow.

As with all things of darkness, the brighter the light, the less they choose to remain in view. Blue morning skies abound now. All is well. Opportunity awaits discovery in this magical city on the southern Florida emerald coast.

Last night, Nicole had chosen not to stay at Rico's place. He had a late-night business meeting regarding another shipment that was coming in from Egypt. One that would most likely, be very profitable. By mutual agreement they both opted to fill the evening with their own company for a change.

Oftentimes, it's healing to be alone. A person can even enjoy it, pleasing only him or herself. Nothing so fulfilling except self-indulgence from food to self-centered, hopes or desires. Nothing to think about but his or her own dreams and in a way, it was good for Rico to have some time to himself. After all he had allot to think about lately. New emotions stirred inside him now. Almost wild and insatiable thoughts of wealth and power, even the power of life and death over other human beings.

Opening the Miami Herald was a morning ritual for Rico. Lots of people now opted for a stint at the laptop each morning to catch up on current affairs. Not so for Rico. Just a good standard hard-copy black and white newspaper that was delivered to his door daily. After all, it had its own odor which often seemed to enhance the taste of his rich self-roasted Colombian coffee.

"It's been two days. I can't believe those fucks wouldn't publish anything as interesting as two murders in South Beach."

"Patience, patience Rico my man" as he turned to page three. Low in the printed columns, there it was. In a small headline halfway down, the page read; Two Found Dead in South Beach.

All things come to those who are willing to do the work and wait he thought.

Two brothers were found dead inside the South Beach public restroom facility early yesterday morning. Police thought it may have stemmed from an argument between the two brothers but were not sure of how it happened. Both men were thought to have been killed by the same handgun further, the police said they would not rule out foul play as separate, identical head wounds may possibly indicate the involvement of a third party.

Rico smiled. Thinking back to what he felt when he pulled the trigger on Gerald. He relived the repeated jolt of the gun. He smelled the burnt gunpowder; He felt and heard the bullets exit the barrel as they sprayed from the muzzle of the gun. Spoken soundly and so deadly yet whispered with a silenced voice.

But the thrill! The shot though the forehead. That was something he would never forget.

Noticing a slight rise in his private's area.

He thought, "Well Rico. You sick Son of a Bitch."

It all happened so fast with H he barely had time to commit it to memory.

It is true, he thought, life departs within seconds upon command when a body is riddled with lead.

Regardless, he seemed to be getting off on Xing Gerald and H. "It's too bad Gerald was so fucking stupid. He ended up getting his brother H killed and I actually, kind of liked him."

The alarm sounded from his cell phone. Time to check on the shipment coming in from Egypt.

Chapter Eighteen: Pros and Cons

"Curt, these guys that assaulted Beth and I were pros I'm telling you. Jolene countered. The way they acted; this isn't the first time they've done something like this. They were completely organized. They knew exactly what they were doing. Maybe part of some gang or something."

"I did manage to bust one of them in the face with my elbow and break his fucking nose."

"How do you know that you broke his nose Jolene?" Curt asked.

"Cause I heard it crack when my elbow hit him, and I saw the mother fuckers blood squirt out of the eyes of the mask he was wearing."

"Dam Girl! Well done. Good for you but, if he is pissed about it, he might try to take it out on Beth. I pray to God, not."

"Why didn't you just call me with your cell phone from the parking lot when it happened? Maybe we could have followed them."

"I couldn't find my cell phone. I looked everywhere and besides; they were gone in a heartbeat."

"You still can't find your cell phone?"

"No, I know I had it with me when I left softball practice because I called one of my friends."

"After the roust, I couldn't find it. I'm pretty sure it was in my purse, but it could have been in my rear pants pocket. Seems I put there allot for convenience anymore. I searched the entire parking lot too."

"OK, you say one of the men picked you up and threw you into the van? Then you cracked him in the face and you both fell out of the van's side door?"

"Yep, that's exactly what I said and that's exactly what happened."

"Jolene, when that guy picked you up from behind and threw you into the van, if your phone was in your rear pocket, could it have come out of your pocket and landed inside the truck when you managed to escape."

"I guess it's possible. Hell, after what happened to us tonight, I guess anything's possible."

"Seriously, that maybe the only way to find those bastards, if we only had someone that knew how to track a cell phone. Do you keep your GPS on or use it to find your way around town?"

"I do indeed." Jolene countered.

"Well, if the GPS and location feature on your phone is on, all we have to do is find someone that can track it. But who knows how to do that? I sure as hell don't."

"I know just the guy." Jolene said, "and he's right here at school too."

"There's no way that I'm going to be able to sleep tonight. Let's get on it.

"Ok, call the police and try to see if they have any suggestions. After all they deal with this kind of thing on a regular basis."

Curt picked up his phone and dialed 911.

"Sheriff's department what is the nature of your call?"

"I'd like to report a kidnapping please."

"Hold the line sir."

Curt waited for no more than 15 seconds.

"Sherriff's department, John Graywolf speaking."

"Yes, hello, this is Curt Lafferty in Cape Coral. My girlfriend was just abducted by some guys in a dark colored van from the FSW faculty parking lot."

"Are you an eyewitness to this kidnapping?"

"No, but Jolene Campbell, her best friend is. She's standing right here."

"Mr. Lafferty, I'm the only one on duty right now, but if you'll give me your address, I'll get right on over there, so we can try to get a lead on this."

"Absolutely." Curt said.

Curt nervously paced the floor and swore that a lifetime had passed since he hung up the phone. Forty minutes had passed before the deputy finally arrived at his house.

Curt and Jolene welcomed the Lee County Deputy upon his arrival.

Deputy John Graywolf, Deputy for the Lee County Sherriff's department for the past five years. A husky man of native American decent. Formerly a member of the Miccosukee Indian Tribal Police Force, John vacated the Miccosukee tribal position after he was denied the opportunity to investigate the murder of his own wife and child. They had been held captive themselves and were killed when the raid to save them went bad.

Authorities expressed feelings of doubt that John could remain objective on the case with the loss of such close family members. It was true. John had lost a great part of his life. He would never be the same, but life goes on. Concurrently, the Lee County

Sheriff's department was in need of a good man, so John Graywolf took the position as Deputy Sherriff. The crimes against his wife and child were solved shortly after he left tribal for which he was grateful. However, he was denied the satisfaction of pursuing and capturing the perpetrators and bringing them to justice himself. Their assailants were tried, found guilty and placed on death row where they currently awaiting execution but, that would not bring back John Graywolf's family.

"I understand what you are feeling Mr. Lafferty. I understand exactly. I lost my wife and child to a situation very similar to this." Deputy Graywolf said.

"I'm so sorry to hear that officer. Please, call me Curt, just call me Curt, if you would Sir."

"Certainly."

John went momentarily silent, starring down at the floor. Through memory he recalled the sight of his wife Dayla's, beautiful face. He smelled the scent of her skin; he felt the passion of her kiss. He saw his 5-year-old daughter Skyla, running towards him. He felt the tug of her little arms hug tightly around his neck. Since the day of their passing, John has fought for sanity, for closure. Outwardly and daily he functions well enough but, inside he persecutes and blames himself for their deaths. A feeling of torment constantly reminds him of the loss of the ones he loved.

Why couldn't he save them? He was a good lawman, why wasn't he there to prevent their abduction. Why! Each day, he played the same old tapes in his mind over and over, never finding the answer to any of the questions that would satisfy and relieve the guilt he carried inside.

John shook his head slightly, as if to clear his thoughts, then re-joined the conversation.

Curt looked at Jolene and raised an eyebrow as if to say, did you catch that?

Jolene nodded and shrugged slightly.

The Deputy continued to take notes during the interrogation of Jolene regarding exactly what had happened.

Deputy Graywolf spoke; "The problem with this is information, we have nothing whatsoever to go on. No leads and the other side of the river to the north has some pretty rough neighborhoods. There's no telling where they took her and the first 24 hours are crucial."

"Look." Curt said, "we may have one chance. God be with us on this. There's an outside possibility that Jolene's cell phone may have fallen out of her pocket inside the van during the scuffle when they tried to get her. She says she had it before it all happened and hasn't seen it since. If they haven't discovered it and it's still on, we may be able to track it down."

"Interesting." Graywolf said, "Our office has tracked phones on numerous occasions. Problem is; we have no one on duty tonight with that kind of experience or ability. Did you try calling it?"

"No, we didn't want them to find it if it's in the truck. It's the only thread of hope we have to go on. A thin thread but at least it's something."

"Sure, we know someone." Jolene piped I, "and we're going to call him. Would you be willing to wait around here till we get ahold of him?"

"Absolutely," Graywolf said.

Chapter Nineteen: The Package

"So, you were able to pick up the package?"

"Yes, Sir we did. No problem."

"Did you find anything that I might be interested in?"

"We searched the package like you asked us to do. We found the usual crap in her purse, but we also found a letter. It may even have some sort of code in it. I mean, I can't make out what it's trying to say but, I think it's definitely something you are going to be interested in. The note was signed by some guy named Ohio Jim."

"Ohio Jim? No Shit? For God's sake hold onto that letter for me. That may be the jackpot that I was looking for. When you picked the package up, anyone recognize any of you? Any of your soldiers?"

The Lead kidnapper hesitated. Thinking to himself. "Did anyone see us? No, Not to my knowledge. No one even saw what happened except the bitch that broke Tommie's nose. I'm sure as hell aren't going to tell him that. I'm not going to let anything jeopardize or get in the way of us getting our money." He may make up some bullshit excuse why, all of a sudden, he doesn't want to pay us. Why it's only worth half now. No, He doesn't need to know any more than I tell him and that's all he's gonna get. He'll only get what I tell him."

Back into the conversation; "Not to my knowledge, we all had masks on, it was dark, and we got a blindfold on her as soon as we got away in the truck."

"Good work. Look, its 1:00 am here, I can be there at your place by, say 8–8:30am in the morning. You at the same place?"

"Yeah man, we are all here and we'll be waiting on you. You going to bring the money?"

"I am indeed and by the way. Make sure the package is all in one piece. I don't want it damaged. I may need what's inside the memory bank. Understand what I'm saying?"

"I do, I read you loud and clear Captain. Loud and Clear."

The call went silent as Rico nervously moved about the room.

"A note from Ohio Jim eh? It could hold the very clues I need to find the treasure. I wish he would have told me a little bit about what it said. Dammit, I should have asked him but, then again. That little son of a bitch may have detected some urgency in my voice and, suddenly, wanted more money. I've got no less than four and a half hours of windshield time between here and there. The code he referred to would have been a good thing for me to focus on to pass the time. Maybe I could figure it out. Perhaps...

No, I'm not calling him back. I'll just wait. I'll have it soon enough. I have to stay ahead of these guys or somehow, I have a feeling they might try to get one over on me if I seem too anxious. Their attitude will change once they see the color of the money. They'll be thinking about it instead of me. I think it will work out just fine the way I left it. It's going to be a long drive tonight."

Rico drove through the night and made the last turn that led to the Ft Myers hideout at 7:05 AM. He parked the car about a quarter block away from where they held Beth.

Rico got out of the car, put on an unusual flat brimmed hat, then donned a pair of wraparound sunglasses, picked up a medium sized gym bag, got out and locked the Ferrari. He barked the alarm on the Fob as he and walked away and headed towards the side door of the building.

Three quick knocks summoned a response from behind the door. "What's the best fruit in Florida?"

"Grapefruit you son of a bitch let me in." Rico replied.

The door opened.

"Did you bring the money?"

Rico threw the bag at the guy that was asking. "It's all there my friend. All green, unsorted and completely spendable. No one is looking for this stash. It came from an old lady and her husband. Cash has its benefits. No questions asked is the normal statement that goes along with it."

Where's the letter you found?

"Here Dude. It's right here. Glad you paid the money up front. It shows your good intentions."

"The Lead Kidnapper handed him the letter."

Rico unfolded it, read and studied the contents of the written text.

"There is no doubt that this is a coded message. Where do you have the girl?"

"She's tied to a chair, right there in the corner of the room over there, you can't miss her."

"I want to talk to her for a few moments. Give me a handkerchief. I'm going to tie it around my face, I want it to muffle my voice. "

"Here. Knock yourself out Dude."

Rico made his way over to where she was and saw Beth slumped over, tied to the chair.

"Excuse me. Are you OK?"

Beth stirred instantly and mumbled incoherently.

"Now, I want to talk to you so, in order to do that I'm going to have to take this piece tape off your mouth. It might sting just a little bit when I take it off, but I'll do the best I can with it. Also, I'm warning you, if you go into some sort of screaming fit, these guys back there on the other side of the room will, no doubt, slap another strip of tape back over your mouth so, I wouldn't do that if I were you. Understand."

Beth nodded her head indicating that she understood.

Rico removed the tape as best he could in order not to cause any undue pain.

"There, that ought to do it."

"I'm so thirsty. "Beth gasped," I've got to have some water. Please give me some water."

"Hey Poncho, bring me a bottle of cold water. Now!"

The shorter of the two gang members lifted a bottle from the garage fridge and handed it to Rico.

Rico unscrewed the lid. "OK, I'm going to hold it up to your lips so, here it comes."

Beth gulped eagerly at the plastic bottleneck.

"Slow down, I'll give you as much as you want. There's plenty."

"Thank You, I was so thirsty. Who are you?"

"That's not important but, what is important is that I have some questions I want to ask you about this letter. The one signed by the guy named Ohio Jim."

"Hey, I've had this blindfold over my eyes for hours. I could barely breath and I'm fucking tired. They wouldn't even let me go to the bathroom. I had to pea my pants because those sons a bitches wouldn't let me go to the bathroom and I'm not in the mood for 40 questions."

Thinking instantly that it may be better for her to cooperate, Beth said; "Look. I only met Ohio Jim one time. He showed up at my office and showed me a coin of sorts and asked me to help him find out what it was. I agreed to try to help him. The next things I find out is that he's been shot to death. Then, the letter came to me at the office the same day we found out about him dying. Are you the one that killed him?"

"No. No I didn't. I'm sorry to hear about your friend." Rico said.

"He wasn't my friend. I told you, I only met him once. Beth continued, I found out that the coin that he had may have come from Colombia South America as far back as the 1500's. Possibly as part of a lost shipment of Spanish gold. But we couldn't prove it."

"Jim said he had a bad feeling about a phone call asking about the coin so, he said he sent me the letter in case something happened to him. I read what he had written but, it didn't make sense to me."

"Please, let me go, I don't know anything more than I've just told you."

"All in good time Mam."

"What is Jennis?" Rico asked

"It's not what, it's who? Jennis was his wife. She passed away in Hurricane Charlie."

"Oh...Ok. So, he loved his Darling Jennis. But the word DARLING is written in all Caps."

"Look, I have no idea about it and frankly I don't give a dam about any of this. I have nothing to do with any of it."

"Ok, OK just hold on a minute. A tiny key will unlock the treasure."

"Look, Like I told you I have no idea what that means either."

"As far as that bullshit about what we held is with the dollars in my house. I don't have a clue on that one either. If anything was there; don't you think the police would have found it? Ask them dammit. I want to go home."

Beth broke out into uncontrollable sobbing which shocked Rico. Even though he was cold hearted at times, he still carried a soft spot in his heart for a beautiful woman.

Rico stood up. "I'm leaving now. Do You want some more water?"

Beth continued to cry.

Rico walked across the garage area to where two of the men were setting at a makeshift table. He pulled the handkerchief off his face, held his finger up to his lips as he said "shhhh," as if to indicate whatever they said would be done so in a whisper.

"I'm taking off now, but I want you to hold her until I return. Probably somewhere around 24 hours is my guess. Hell, I haven't slept forever but... I'll be back soon and look, give her something to eat and some water to drink too and for God's sake, let her go to the bathroom. Oh, and one more thing, no one lays a finger on the girl. No One. Understand? I hate loose ends but, I may need to talk to her again. If anything happens to her it will come from my hand, not yours. You Got It?"

"Got it." Said the Lead kidnapper.

Rico, put on his sunglasses and the large hat, opened the door and exited towards his car.

Chapter Twenty: Patty Tech Nerd

Patrick William Morrow III, also, known, lovingly, by his friends as Patty.

A highly intelligent tech nerd, friend and gopher to FSW. He didn't have a mean bone in his body. Tall, slight of build, he sported red hair and greenish eyes. Patty is an absolute "electronic techno" whiz. He also had a habit of quoting old song lyrics to describe daily situations which was, at times, very entertaining.

A trust baby, well off, seemingly a lifelong student in the Archeology department with no real outside ambition. Patty was always willing to help the undergraduate classmates with their studies. Doing odd jobs around the school, he made himself available for projects that were needed by the Archeology and Geological departments.

Patty Loved Beth. Their friendship had grown platonically over the past five years as he had given her a hand on numerous onsite digs, whenever she was the overseer.

Whenever new computers or electronic equipment of any kind were delivered on campus, seems it was always Patty who was first to arrive upon the scene hoping that he would be nominated to set up the new components and bring them to life. He loved it. He had partial training in electronics but most of his knowledge was kinetic. For the most part he remained fairly quiet and didn't talk much mentioning occasionally that he would rather hear the sound of a well manipulated computer keyboard than he would to hear the sound of his own voice. He had a big heart too.

"Jolene, can you get Patty on the phone?"

"His number was in my phone and I don't know it. I know. Let me call the school paging service and have him call us."

"Well, get on it girl."

Jolene put in for the page. Now the trio just waited as the moments ticked by.

They all jumped when Curt's cell phone rang.

"I hope that's him." Curt said.

"Jolene, you answer it, please."

"Hello, this is Jolene Campbell."

"Jolene, Hi, this is Patty, you paged me?"

"I did Patty, Somethings come up and we are in desperate need of your skills. Where are you?"

"I'm in Orlando. What's up?"

"Beth Higgins has been kidnapped."

"Oh, Wow, No Way!"

"I wish it weren't so Patty but, I'm afraid it's true."

"Have you called the Police? What do you want me to do? How can I help with a kidnapping?"

"Patty, we need you to track my cellphone. We think it may have fallen out in the van that the gang took her a way in. Can you do that?"

"I dam sure can. I've done it before but I'm at least three hours away from you, plus, I'll have to go to my house and pick up my laptop before I can even meet with you."

"Patty, I'm asking you with all my heart to drop what you're doing and help us. We need you tonight more than ever."

"I'm on it. I'm out of here." Patty said. "Text me the address where I should meet you and I'll see you in 4 hours max."

"Thanks Patty, I knew we could count on you. Be careful. It's going to be a long, late night drive."

Jolene clicked the cell phone into silence. Then texted Patty Curt's address to the number he had called from.

Jolene turned to the men; "Considering the time now, it looks like he won't be here until around 8:30 in the morning."

"God that's a lifetime." Curt said, wrenching his fists together.

"Deputy Graywolf, are you willing to stay with us till Patty gets here?"

"Absolutely, I'll be glad to help, I can't let this one go."

Curt invited Graywolf and Jolene to use his home as though it were their own. Make yourself comfortable he said.

Curt retired to his recliner chair in the living room.

"I'll never make it till 8:30 in the morning he thought. I'm upset. I'm so fucking pissed off and afraid for Beth all in the same emotion. He thought to himself. I don't know how I can deal with all this. But, I must. I have to calm down otherwise, I'll be no help to Beth at all. I can't believe I could wait my whole lifetime to fall in love just have it taken away overnight. I feel so dam helpless."

Helpless, there's that dam word again. It can be and is usually defined as a lonely empty feeling. A situation presenting itself as one without hope.

How could he help Beth best at this particular minute? What could he possibly do for her to improve the situation?

Staring at the floor, he lifted his line of sight to the back of the leather recliner in front of him. His mind drifted, failing to separate reality from fantasy, he found himself at the crash site on the desert battlefield in Iraq. He remembered the pain threshold above all believability. Partially delusional, it was as though the Apache gunship controls loomed there in front of him. Flight gauges lined the back of chair. Extending his hand, he tried to touch the machine gun activation control button on the flight stick. Would it work? Could he possibly protect himself and shoot his way out if he needed too? Could this change the outcome? He tried again waving his hand towards them.

"Dammit! Just out of reach."

Besides, none were working. Nothing to aid his escape in the enviable event the enemy showed up before his buddies could mount a rescue.

Helplessness. A useless, empty feeling that serves no purpose nor offers a positive solution. A complete waiting state of mind in an empty room where tapes of possible outcomes are played over and over ending with the same fruitless result. Like seeking direction with a bladeless compass. Like a blinded man finding a pair of reading glasses. Like hearing an incessant ringing with no phone or communications headset in sight.

Curt felt completely helpless. There he was, as when he was confined to the chopper cockpit after the crash, trapped in his own living room, longing to help the new-found love of his life yet, finding himself consumed by an empty volume of despair which offered no options and no solutions.

Looking down at his leg feeling the pain. Seeing the bone sticking up through his bloody flight suit, yet not being able to move to a more comfortable position. This was the same totally helpless feeling.

Even though he possessed many skills and abilities, he could think of nothing to improve the moment. He remembered, the noises and that his sense of hearing became much improved as the wreckage of his craft prevented him from seeing anything outside of the cockpit. Complete concentration centered upon each sound, every vibration, every bin was evaluated through the single sense which continued to yield nothing. Even recognizable noises can play tricks on a stressed mind. Would he be saved, or would the enemy find him helplessly confined inside the chopper wreckage. Would they kill him? Would they set the wreckage ablaze while he was trapped helplessly inside?

"As God is My Witness, if I get through this, I will never allow myself to become helpless again. Dear God, please keep Beth safe. Cause a fruitful end to what appears to me now to be a totally helpless situation. AMEN LORD."

Regaining composure, Curt looked up and asked; Graywolf; "Will there be other Sherriff's cars brought in when the tracking begins in the morning?"

"Probably not he said. It's totally against protocol but, that's exactly the reason my wife and daughter were killed when they tried to rescue them. The Tribal force went blazing up to where they were held with the sirens blaring which alerted the men holding them. Used as shields, when gunfire erupted, they ended up getting killed in the crossfire. I don't want this to go down that way if this proves to be a worthwhile lead. Surprise is always a plus to have on our side."

"Hell! We could be wasting time right now if that dam phone isn't in the kidnapper's truck or if they already found it."

Time passed slowly, however at 8:15 AM Patty knocked on Curt's front door. Everyone inside jumped as Curt scurried to answer it.

"Patty, we're so thankful that you came. We are so grateful. Please help us."

"Ok, gottcha, you bet, I'm glad to do it."

"Give me a few moments to make some updates and do a couple of downloads. Patty proceeded to bring up a grid map on the screen and localize it to their specific geographical area."

143

With blazing speed Patty's fingers ripped through the laptop keyboard sounding like a tiny machine gun in rapid fire. Then, with a final single finger slam.

"Got it. He said."

Chapter Twenty-One: God Help Us!

Patty looked up and smiled. "Now to activate the tracking program sequence. Jolene, give me your phone number."

Patty entered 555 937 8818 into the program.

"Loading! You were right Jolene. I'm getting a signal. Your phone is still on. I've got it, I've got it! I'm in." Patty exclaimed. "Obviously, your phone must have been dumped in the truck during the fight and so far, no one's detected it. I've got a signal coming in from across the river and it's actually not that far from here. First things first." Patty said.

"I'm going to silence the ringer in the phone and kill the light system, so it doesn't give its position away. Then, let's cross correlate Google maps satellite view with this signal into the program with an overlay. Got it. I Got it." Patty said enthusiastically.

"Let's take a closer look." Patty zoomed in. "The Satellite view looks like some sort of garage on the end of that abandoned shopping center. See it? Jolene, does that vehicle look familiar?"

Jolene walked in behind and looked over Patty's shoulder at the laptop screen.

"Curt, John That's the truck for sure. I can just see the top of it behind that fence, but I'd bet anything that's the truck they used. Beth, just about, has to be inside that building."

Deputy Graywolf turned towards Curt and asked; "Do you have a gun?"

Curt replied. "I sure as hell do."

"Good." he said.

Graywolf stood up and began to motion with his hands.

"Here's the plan. We are going to quietly make the building and see if we can somehow get in without making a bunch of noise."

"I'm going too." Jolene spoke up. "I'm not much on guns but pretty good with this ball bat."

John just smiled. "Not my weapon of choice but, if it works for you, it'll have to do." Looking at the bat; "Does that thing have two barrels on it?" The deputy kidded.

"If I swing it fast enough it does." Jolene said. "By the way, thinking back to earlier this evening, I didn't see a gun on any of them."

"Patty are you..."

"Not on your life. This is way out of my league. I love Beth to pieces but, I'm staying in the car. You'll thank me later. Hell, I'd probably get in your way anyhow."

"Ok, OK. Let's roll. Patty will that set-up continue to operate real time once we're on the road."

"Yes Sir. I've got an unlimited data plan so no problem whatsoever."

"Curt, I'd suggest taking your car. I'd hate for them to catch wind that a Sherriff's cruiser was in their neighborhood. Patty, you set up front, so you can tell us which streets to take."

"Great by me. Let's do it."

The four of them piled in Curt's Jeep.

Curt looked back at Graywolf through the rear-view mirror and said; "I dam near got a two door when I bought this thing. Tonight, I am so glad I didn't. It's four doors or nothing for me from now on."

Curt backed out of his driveway and headed to the Cape Bridge intersection, then made a left-hand turn. Traffic was moving at a normal pace as they crossed the big river bridge.

"Take the next ramp to the right." Patty said. "The one that says McGregor, then left at the light. It looks like five, no six blocks then we'll want to take another right. I'll let you know.

"Ok, now, in one block we are going to turn right again and that will put us on the road leading straight to the building. The truck will be at the end of the fence."

Curt made the turn to meet a car passing them going in the opposite direction.

"I'd say that's pretty dam unusual. A Ferrari in this neighborhood?"

"Could be a drug deal. " Graywolf said. "This area is known for being the wrong place to be in."

"Slow down Curt, it's right there in front of us." Patty pointed.

"I see it. Jolene, is that the van?"

"Dam Skippy." she said. "That's it for sure."

"I pray to God that Beth is OK." Curt muttered.

Graywolf spoke up. "Ok, ease the car over to the right here and let's get out. Curt, slide the gun body back and put a live shell into the chamber. Leave it cocked. The only thing I want between you and that thing going off is a touch of your finger."

"Sounds good to me." Curt said.

Deputy Graywolf jacked a shell into the chamber of his gun also. Proceeding forward, he held his hand high pointing his weapon upward.

"Let's make our way over to that side door. With any luck we can get the door open without any major problems. If I have to shoot the door open, I will. Hopefully that doesn't happen that way or we'll lose the element of surprise."

"Jolene stay close behind us."

The trio walked towards the side door of the building. Upon reaching it, John tapped on the steel window enclosure.

The guy inside said; "Did you forget something man?"

Graywolf replied, "Ah, yeah sorry man and then mumbled incoherently."

Graywolf opened his mouth as if surprised and looked back towards Curt. Then nodded his head as the door started to open.

As the man inside peeked around to look out. Graywolf grabbed him by the throat and pulled him outside. His face looked flushed, his nose looked red and somewhat swollen. Graywolf held his gun hand up as the man tried to grab for it. The Deputy struggled to sling the guy down to the ground.

From out of nowhere, with all her might, like she was swinging for a low inside fast ball, Jolene cut down hard with the aluminum bat across the outside of the gang members knee, crushing the tendons on the outside of his leg.

He went down screaming.

"YOU! You Bitch, I'll."

Thunk. With a quick wrist over of the aluminum bat, Jolene cracked him squarely over the head. He went out like a light, then he slumped to the ground.

Seizing the opportunity, Graywolf and Curt rushed inside.

"Lee County Sherriff." Graywolf yelled. "Put your hands up so I can see them."

One of the gang jumped up to Graywolf's right side pointing an automatic pistol at him. In a blistering move, Graywolf swung around raising his weapon, instantly pulling the trigger of Glock 40, boom-boom, twice hitting him dead center of the chest. The gang member reeled backwards and fell, crashing through a stash of supplies and boxes.

The sound of the exploding pistol charges inside the garage was deafening, Beth screamed and kicked to free herself. Trying to get loose from the zip ties around her wrists. Struggling, her chair fell over as she found herself laying on her side. Behind the fallen gang member, another one of the kidnappers rose and shot once at Graywolf.

As though he was making his way through a police training maze. Methodically, Graywolf took the second guy out instantly with two more shots. Boom-Boom!

Curt saw Beth across the room tied to a chair blindfolded. He ran to her as the lead kidnapper headed in her direction also.

As Graywolf raised his gun, on the other side of Beth, two shots from an automatic pistol rang out. Graywolf staggered.

Curt fired four times knocking the lead man backwards where he collapsed on the floor. Boom, boom-boom-boom. Curt quickly turned and pointed his smoking gun to cover the man to make sure he was no threat.

Curt yanked the blindfold off Beth's forehead and kissed her. "Oh Beth, Beth Honey, Are you ok? I was so worried about you. I'm so thankful you're alive."

Curt Caressed and hugged her.

He looked upwards; "Oh My God, Thank You Lord for protecting her."

Curt glanced back over to where John Graywolf had fallen on the floor of the garage.

"Jolene, cut these ties off Beth, help us. Get her free now."

Curt jumped over a floor jack and ran to where Graywolf was laying.

"John, John! What's wrong? John. You hit? JOHN......."

Curt, I'm alright. Did we save them? Did we make it in time? Are they ok?

Curt cradled John in his arms to support him. Curt saw the distant stare in Graywolf's eyes.

Apparently at least one of the lead man's bullets had penetrated through the armhole of Graywolf's bulletproof vest and into his chest. Blood ran down the side of his uniform.

Curt realized instantly what was going on. Knowing that John was horribly wounded he was having problems separating fact from fantasy. A drop of blood trickled from John's nose.

"Yes! You saved them John. You saved them both."

"You're a hero. You got nothing to worry about now John. It's over now. It's finally over. We are all so grateful to you."

John attempted a smile as he coughed. From his mouth a fine spray of blood came forth and hit the floor. No sooner had he coughed again than his eyes glazed into a distant stare.

"Jolene." Curt screamed. "Call an ambulance. Now. Call the police too and tell them there's an officer down. Don't waste a second. Beth will be ok, right now we gotta get help for John. Stay with me John. Stay with me."

John was limp and unresponsive. Curt looked up as if to receive instructions from above then looked back down.

Curt closed Graywolf's eyelids with a gentle nudge of his thumb and fore finger. "Rest well my friend. You deserve it."

Within minutes, with sirens blaring, the police and ambulance arrived almost concurrently.

Beth, Jolene and Curt had made their way outside and were standing next to the building with Patty.

The Lee county Sherriff's car stopped in front of Curt's jeep. An officer driving stepped out and moved towards Curt.

"Anyone hurt inside?"

"Yeah, Three men, they're 10-7, all dead."

"Graywolf took'em out." "Graywolf, questioned the officer? John Graywolf is here?"

"Yes, Curt said. I'm afraid Officer Graywolf is down too. He was hit during the fight; I was holding him in my arms when he died. He was a very brave man!"

"That's the problem with these gangs related incidents, almost no one comes out alive when shit like this happens. The officer quickly waved the paramedics inside to where John lay."

Outside, Jolene kept watch over the only surviving gang member.

Somewhat still in a daze, he regained consciousness. looking around, he demanded. "What about me?"

"What about you?" the officer replied. "Did you shoot my friend?"

"No, I didn't have a dam thing to do with any of it. I swear. I was outside. I don't even have a gun. I didn't have anything to do with any of it."

"Yeah Right." Jolene spoke up. "You kidnapped my best friend."

"No, No wait. It wasn't me. I didn't have anything to do with it. I need some medical attention. Dammit to Hell, I'm gonna sue somebody."

"Shut up you Son of a Bitch. You'll be lucky I don't shoot you myself."

Reluctantly, the officer returned from the second patrol car and directed one of the Paramedics over to attend the fallen gang member.

"Beth, Honey, are you Ok now? Do you need one of these medics to take a look at you."

"No, I'm ok, Curt, You're my hero! That was some rescue. Beth smiled admiringly at Curt then put her arms around his waist and looked up at him. Weren't you scared? It was deafening, Beth said, there was so much noise I swear I thought we were all going to die."

"Truthfully Beth, it all happened so fast there really wasn't time to be scared. Except for worrying about you. The only thing that scared me was worrying about whether or not you'd be hurt."

"Something inside pushed me onward. I would have risked everything. It was definitely touch and go dear, but it had to be done. Thank God, we're all ok. All except for Graywolf that is."

"But You Know? Somehow, I think that he's just fine. I think his wife and daughter are at his side right now. I'm almost positive that he saw them coming towards him as he passed."

With a questioning look on her face, Beth looked away then down.

"He was a brave man Beth. He saved your life."

"I'll never forget this day as long as I live but right now, I'm absolutely, exhausted. I just want to go home. Can we go home now Curt?"

"Oh, wait just a second, Curt, I forgot to tell you. There was someone else, other than these gang members was here this morning. He came to interrogate me about what I knew. He asked about the letter that Ohio Jim sent me and other things. I think he took Jim's letter. Truthfully, I think he is the real gang leader and he's probably the one who had me kidnapped in order to gain access to any information I may have had. He seemed knowledgeable about the possibility of a treasure too."

"He left here just a few minutes before you knocked on the door. You must have seen him as you arrived."

Thinking back to when they saw the Ferrari exiting the neighborhood.

"I wonder." Curt said.

"Look folks, I know this has been quit an ordeal but, you're going to have to come downtown with us to answer some questions."

"Officer, this lady was the one that was kidnapped, she's tired, needs a nap, a shower and some food. How bout I bring her to your office later today say, around 3:00 this afternoon? Will that work for you?"

"Well, I have to call CSI, clean this place up and get these bodies out of here, I think we can work with that." The officer replied. "See you then."

The officer reached into his shirt pocket and retrieved a card. Handing it to Curt. "Here is the address. See You later."

"Ok, Thanks Officer, we appreciate it."

Curt helped Beth into the Jeep. Then Patty and Jolene both piled into the backseat.

Patty spoke up; "It sounded like forty people were killed with all that shooting. Damndest thing I've ever heard."

"It was dam sure loud from my perspective too Patty. It took me back to Desert Shield for sure. Touch and go not knowing if we would make it out or not."

Curt spoke up. "What difference 24 hours can make, let's get out the hell of here while we still can. Everyone's car is at my house except Beth's. We can order in some breakfast when we get there if anyone wants too."

Curt twisted the key to the right as the Jeep's engine spun its way to life.

Once Beth was inside the Jeep, she put her face in her hands, bent forwards over her knees and burst out crying. Curt reached over patted her gently on the back.

"It's ok now baby. You're going to be just fine. No one can hurt you now..."

Chapter Twenty-Two: Is the Doctor In?

Rico always had a pay to play cell phone for use on occasions such as this. He bought two hours use at a time from a small Ma & Pa C store over on south 5th street in Miami and he always registered for the phone with a phony name.

Being on the west end of Alligator alley is certainly not where Rico wanted his cell phone number to be traced to at a time like this. He had turned his I-phone off, midtown before he left Miami.

Near the Naples exit, Rico engaged the second cell phone. The tower picked up the phone indicating a strong signal. Looking down he picked up a piece of paper with a phone number written on it.

Continually glancing up at the road, holding the phone with his fingers, He awkwardly punched in the number with his thumb and waited for the ringer to sound.

A voice at the other end of the line: "Hello."

"Dr. Alvera, Enrique Ribeiro here."

"Ah, oh yes, Hello Rico, what a surprise to hear from you this morning."

"Well, I took a chance on calling you at your house, it being Saturday and all, I didn't think you would be in your office today."

"Ah, No, I'm usually here most weekends. What can I do for you Rico?"

"Dr. Alvera, I've got a letter regarding the treasure. It was written by the man you overheard in the office next to yours."

"Ah, you mean that fisherman who called himself Ohio Jim?"

"Yep, that's the one. Anyway, this letter has some sort of code in it and I was wondering if you would be available today to help me try and decipher it."

"Ah, Oh, Ah how exciting and interesting. Certainly, I would love to."

"I'm actually here in Fort Myers right now. I can come over now if you will give me your address."

"Ah, yes, surely, my residence address is 7462 SW Key Terrace, Fort Myers, Fl 33908."

Rico wrote it down.

"Excellent, shall I bring us some coffee and donuts? Have you had your breakfast yet?"

"Ah, Well no, as a matter of fact. Ah Yes, I think I would like that. Ah, if you are bringing donuts, I especially like the long ones with the crème filling inside."

"You Got It Doc." Rico replied. "Coffee black?"

"Ah, yes. Wonderful, that is most acceptable."

"Good deal then, see you there in a few minutes."

As promised, Rico wasted no time. Within 20 minutes Rico arrived in front of Dr. Alvera's residence.

Gathering his purchases, hands full, he exited the Ferrari carefully closing the door behind him with his knee.

Dr. Alvera awaited his arrival at his front door.

"Ah, Come in Sir, please come in. It's good to see you again Enrique."

"Likewise, Doctor. It's been awhile."

"Ah, yes, it certainly has. Ah, it's been quite a while since I've had a donut, especially one such as you have brought me."

"Yes, Sir and here is your coffee too."

"Ah, Thank You again."

"You are welcome. Dr. Alvera, I've come to enlist your help in solving a riddle. I have some clues that I wish to discern the meaning of."

Rico quickly looked away as he caught a whiff of that same old lingering odor that made itself known in Alvera's presence."

"Ah, clues, you say."

Rico regained his composure and answered. "Yes, clues. I don't know if you know this or not but the fisherman you called Ohio Jim was killed a couple of days ago."

"Oh, no, Ah, I had no idea."

"Yes, I was very sad to hear the news also. However, he left behind some clues which may be very helpful to us if we can determine their meaning."

"I've discovered that before his death he left three clues regarding the possible location of the treasure."

"Ah, Oh, how exciting. The day is young and will afford us much time to talk. I am all ears, please share what you know with me."

"I'm not sure what it's worth or not but this is what I was told."

"The clues in order are; What we held is hidden with the dollars at home."

"A tiny key will unlock the treasure."

"And finally;"

"I miss my DARLING Jennis."

"Ah, Very interesting. If you are asking me my opinion, His statement of "what we held is hidden within the dollars at home", I'd say that the coin he found is most assuredly hidden at his place of residence. Possibly with some other money or valuables."

"Yes, that's kind of what I thought too Professor Alvera, however, the police made no mention of finding anything unusual or of value that they found when they investigated his death and looked through his house. I think the police are usually pretty thorough, aren't they?"

"Ah, yes, usually very thorough."

"Well, what do you make of this clue. A tiny key will unlock the treasure. This clue makes me think he knew for sure that a treasure exists, that he had found it and that he knew exactly what was needed to open it."

"Ah, Yes, it does seem so. Ah, in order for us to separate hot air from space we must first separate whether he is speaking in literal terms or if he is still talking of an analogy."

"Good thinking Doc."

"Ah, as the ideas come to me, let me share these thoughts with you. He is obviously speaking about one of two things. Literally, a key that would unlock a lock as you would lock a treasure chest to prevent access or perhaps, he was speaking possibly of an island or small key as they are known. Would you think? A location if you will. A tiny key or cay as the Spanish originally called them."

"Oh my God, That's brilliant Dr. Alvera. I would have never thought of that."

"Ah, there are many small keys within Pine Island and Matlacha sounds. Perhaps we should look at a local map of the area to see if we can learn anything through geographical locations shown on them."

"Excellent idea. Do you have any sort of local area maps Professor?"

"Ah, it may be within your fortune that I just may be able to produce one. Let's look in my study library and see what we can find. Ah, just as I suspected. Yes, I think this one will do nicely."

"Ah, also, considering the fact that the fisherman lived on the north end of Pine Island and that the legend points to Boca Grande Pass as where the treasure should be located, perhaps we should look between those two places for areas of interest first. If my memory serves me correctly, these two locations nearly oppose each other west to east. We should look to see what we can learn from a map of the area. After all, the Calusa made use of every landmass available in the area for hundreds of years."

"Excellent." Rico replied

"Ah, now what did you say the last clue was? Do you recall?"

"Yes, it's very strange Doc. It's like he's professing his love for his deceased wife, but he describes her as his Darling Jennis and DARLING is spelled with all capital letters."

"Ah ha, this is almost too obvious to me. By accentuating all the letters with capitals, he is making that very word the center focal point of the clue."

"DARLING."

Taking out a pen marker, Professor Alvera drew a line west to east from the northern end of Pine Island over to Boca Grande Pass. He then scoured the map looking intently at all that is presented there.

"Ah, this man was a fisherman and constantly used these waterways. I know from personal experience that the

159

commercial fishing dock is located a mile south of Mid-Point of the island on the Pine Island Sound side. From his house, this fisherman undoubtedly made his way there to work either by car, which does not help us, ah, or almost daily by boat which is a much more logical approach to his routine."

Professor Alvera then made a mark on the map from the commercial fishing dock, mid-point Pine Island North South, to intersect with the east west mark he had previously made on the map.

Scanning along it, they both looked up at each other both stunned and surprised.

Almost in unison they pointed to the map and said, "Oh my God...DARLING key. "

There on the map, along the line that the professor had drawn, was a tiny key just off to the side of the main channel that lead to the commercial fishing docks which was marked Darling Key.

"Ah, I'll bet you that this man went past this small key no less than 10,000 times in his lifetime. To me, this tiny, obscure little key is the prime location for a treasure to have been stored by the Calusa Indians. Too small to be of value to anyone. Not large enough for anyone to have made use of for any real purpose. Possibly a tiny karst, limestone remnant that may well have been utilized for a special purpose by the Indians back when the legend started. A Tiny Key or cay as we know them to have been called, back then, unlocks the treasure and I love my darling Jennis, DARLING being all in caps. This map concludes that this must be the location exactly being described by both clues."

"Professor, I believe you have solved the riddle. Excellent work Sir. I think the treasure must lie within that tiny key, perhaps hidden for hundreds of years without a single soul suspecting that anything whatsoever of value was contained within."

"Ah, Excellent. If so, then perhaps you can see your way to upping the percentage of my compensation."

"Absolutely Professor. Absolutely. I'll make sure you get everything that is coming to you."

Rising from the Study table. Rico could hardly control himself. He briefly paced the floor then turned; "Professor would you like another donut?"

"Ah, yes please. They are very good."

As Rico came closer, he was barely able to tolerate the smell that immitted from the hermit like old schoolteacher. Sickening would be a better word for it. " Why would a school like FSW allow a stinking Son of a Bitch like this man even to teach there?" Rico thought to himself.

Upon his arrival, the odor permeated the area even out onto the porch where he first sensed it. "God, I forgot just how much this Mother Fucker stinks. Fuck this shit he thought."

Rico leaned partially over Alvera's shoulder and laid the box of donuts in front of the Professor on the study table.

"Go ahead, please, enjoy."

As Professor Alvera lifted the lid and surveyed the contents inside the box, Rico deliberately stepped to Alvera's side. Reaching into his coat pocket, Rico pulled out a large syringe, yanked off the needle cap. Then he plunged the injection heavily into the side Alvera's neck.

The force must have hit a spinal nerve as Alvera seemed to be mostly paralyzed upon impact. Slumping forward towards the table he could only manage to eke out an incoherent grunting sound.

"Yes, sir Professor, I'm going to make sure you get everything that is coming to you. Thanks for the help. I know you know how I hate loose ends and you are one loose end I just can't afford to have hanging around."

Rico had mercilessly stuck Professor Alvera with and injection of Succinyl Choline Chloride in solution. A chemical sometimes used during surgical operations yet in large doses it becomes a deadly agent instantly paralyzing all involuntary bodily functions including breathing and heartbeat. Mysteriously, then within an hour or so, the compound simply dissolves away to harmless salts. Mostly undetectable if an autopsy is initiated, unless, of course, it was specifically looked for.

Considering the fact that this was Saturday, it should be at least couple of days before anyone would think to find him missing. That would certainly change the scene of his expiration as well as any evidence found at the sight.

After cleaning the room to remove all trace of his ever being there, crushing the paper cup he drank from into his jacket pocket, Rico quickly exited the scene, leaving it to look as though the victim's heart had merely given out. It would be very hard to detect otherwise.

Surely, No one would see the single tiny puncture wound in Professor Alvera's neck.

With his head laid partially sideways down upon the study table, saliva drooled from his open mouth. His eyes stared distantly forward as though looking for another chance at life. One that would not be forthcoming.

Heavy lines accented all about his facial features. Fleshy bags under his eyes were accented by partially unshaven jowls. His hair smoothed back, indicated an absence of shampooing and a large dark mole sprouted from beside his left nostril. Alvera was a very unattractive man in his mid–sixties, very unkept and the SMELL. Yes, the smell that lingered constantly around him, who would possibly suspect anything other than an expired heart, simply a natural occurrence. Certainly no one would want to

162

spend any extra time on the corpse such as this to determine anything contrary to the obvious.

Rico quickly folded up the map Alvera had provided and headed out of the house. Upon reaching the front door Rico stopped briefly, turned and looked back over his shoulder. "I hope you enjoyed the donuts you stinking pig. I ought to send you a bill for the home delivery service. Have a nice rest, won't you?"

"I'm going treasure hunting now Doc. I'll let you know how it turns out."

Rico spun the center main door handle lock from inside, quietly closed it behind him, then casually moved in the direction of the Ferrari.

Chapter Twenty-Three: A Tight **Squeeze**

Gulls, overhead, called out to one another as if to announce that an intruder was coming into the area. As he approached, he noticed that one side of the tiny key had, what appeared to be a sandy beach. Steadily, he paddled the small craft in that general direction. The water was calm allowing him to guide the bow of the boat quietly into the back side of the little island. Upon arrival, to his dismay, he realized that what he thought was sand, was actually bones. Large and small, perhaps animal in original of some sort, he wasn't sure. A few looked as if they had been recently deposited there, left to dry at the shoreline. Others were pulverized. All were bleached white, as if to give off a blinding snow-white glow in the morning sunlight.

Enrique stepped out of the small boat he had borrowed and quickly proceeded to hide it. Grabbing the machete, he brought with him, he chopped down a few mangrove limbs and spread them over the open hull. Adding two more leafy fronds from a close by palm, the craft was now completely obscure. Satisfied that no one would see it, he turned and began to slash his way towards the peak of the limestone key.

Working on a hunch, after and in-depth discussion with Professor Alvera, he came to this tiny key to survey the possibilities of what may lie therein. Today's trip was well planned except for the fact that he had forgotten one of the most important items to have in the Florida bush. Bug-spray! Instantly, upon landing, the No-see-ums attacked him ruthlessly, continually biting. The onslaught was maddening. Finding their way into his ears and into his hair and scalp. No amount of shewing away or scratching provided relief.

For some reason, those dam things always find their way into the eyes too. Perhaps it's the fresh water the eyes contain in an area inundated with unusable saltwater. Perhaps the moisture of his watering eyes was the allure.

Regardless of the reason, they bit him hard on the face too, even forcing their way into his eyebrows and lashes. A large whelp appeared over his right cheekbone. Bloodthirsty, mosquitos inundated and attacked his exposed legs.

Partially blinded by sweat and the no-see-um swarm, Rico, stopped briefly, believing he saw movement through his prereferral vison to his right. He turned to look in that direction but saw nothing.

Glancing upward, his heart began to race. Almost crownlike, atop the apex of the small land mass he could see a number of weathered conch shells lined in a row. Obviously, encased there intentionally in some sort of ancient concrete or permanent binding agent.

"Those didn't get there by nature, he thought, that's manmade."

Rico knew from his talks with Alvera that the Calusa never threw anything away of value. When the opportunity arose, every ship was raided and plundered in order to acquire whatever weapons, tools or raw materials they could salvage. Also, Rico knew that it had to be the Calusa that took away the majority of the treasure, if it existed and he believed it did, after the ship was burned to the waterline per the legend. He knew that the Calusa were clever, utilizing natural structures, vugular, eroded limestone caves or sometimes building shell mounds above the water line instead of attempting to dig large holes to utilize for storage. A natural structure exactly like this little hollow limestone remnant of an island would provide just such a place.

A visual survey of it looked to him as though the conch shell covering was made with great care, each large shell placed there intentionally as a barrier to encase and protect whatever would be held inside.

Renewed with excitement, Rico hacked away at the remaining overgrowth, fighting off the relentless onslaught of the bugs, waving a clearing hand across in front of his face occasionally, squinting to keep the stinging sweat out of his eyes.
Rico chopped feverishly as he inched his way upward through the protective mangrove overgrowth towards his goal.
His foot caught on a mangrove root causing him to stumble, falling partially into the saltwater. Regaining his composure, he scrambled back to his feet.
Once again, he thought he saw movement to his side. But nothing came into to view when he turned to look in that direction.
"I hope that fucking Alvera knew what he was talking about or this is all going to be for nothing." Rico said breathlessly.
Completing two more slashes with the two-foot blade of the machete brought him to the base of the structure. A Limestone outcrop that had indeed, been altered. That's right altered by man, almost house like. What could be hidden inside if not something of value.

Rico glanced to the eastern side of the structure where the morning light was shining the brightest. There he saw a weathered hole in the upper shell wall about 6" wide which, perhaps, would allow him to see inside.

Crawling up, peaking in, he saw wonderful color.
"It's GOLD he screamed. I found it! I Fucking found it!"

Rico reached out toward the hole. Movement to his side again distracted him. He looked up and to his right where a giant serpentine form appeared. Its massive head held high above him, poised and ready to strike.

Instinctively, Rico raised the machete, but his move was much too slow for defense. Omitting a vicious hissing noise, the massive snake struck out, grabbing his arm. The razorlike teeth of the snake penetrated painfully, deep into his forearm. Dropping the machete, he screamed. With lighting like efficiency, the massive snake flopped four heavy coils of its body over and looped around Rico's upper torso down to his legs. A fifth coil found its way up and around his throat. He gasped.

The snake had trapped Rico beneath the coils and pinned his arms to his side, there was no fighting back. Terrified, he cried out. Caught in the death grip of this incredibly unforgiving force of nature, Rico felt the air leave his lungs wheezing past his larynx. Struggling, against the inevitable, every attempt he made to breathe was met with an even greater tightening coil pressure by the serpent.

Completely unable to move, mostly paralyzed, Rico stared into the eyes of his assailant. Sinister slotted pupils separated the copper colored iris of its large eyes. Eyes held high in its massive head returned his gaze with a piercing, uncaring dedication. The distinct, almost camouflage like markings of the snake's body had become distorted, its skin stretched near the limit of the

167

coils crushing capability. Relentless, the snake would not ease its grip.

Blood ran from Rico's nose. Now bulging from their sockets, the effects of this incredible, externally applied force caused the tiny blood vessels in Rico's eyes to break.

With a loud crunch, Rico's pelvis snapped. He squeaked out a tiny yelp. A dull, low level sound of pressed air and liquid escaped from his anus. Determined to keep its prey in check, the snake applied even greater pressure. Bones in Rico's ribcage snapped like dry twigs as Frigate birds circled above. It would prove to be the last thing Rico would ever see.

Only a few minutes had passed since the snake's first strike yet, in that short time everything had changed. Human life is a fragile commodity, held precariously within the body it was born unto. Both a finite resource at best. The two can be separated, one from the other, in no more than a few seconds.

The life that was once so full and vibrant was now extinguished. Thoughts of his girlfriend, his Ferrari, the business in Miami, his parents and his life had been turned off like an electrical switch.

Personal gain and possessions would play no part in his life now. His life was over.

Greed does strange things to a person. Sometimes making a man take chances that normal thought processes would not allow. Tragically the lives, he himself, had so ruthlessly taken, in the attempt to recover the treasure, were now all for naught also. The fact is, regardless of all the wealth and holdings a man has acquired in his lifetime, the soul is the only tangible remnant of existence there is left to be taken into the here-after.

Blinded by greed which became an obsession, the wealth he sought would never come to fruition. No loose ends here.

His sentence had now been read and handed down. Karma was both Judge and Jury. Together they had extracted their own natural form of justice. The clever, manipulating man everyone once called the Miami Flash was now dead. Never to be heard from again.

As it is documented historically, many times gold extracts a heavy price when pursued, even more so once it is found. The Treasure of Boca Grande Pass had already claimed many human lives. When would it end?

Why would such a deadly creature be found in Florida? That being the mighty Anaconda, the largest snake in to be found the world. It is certainly not an indigenous species to the state of Florida. Rather an Invasive life form that should never have been found in the local wilds. Early on, perhaps it was someone's fascination with this deadly creature. Possibly an illegal purchase from an exotic pet store. Small enough to be kept in a cage or climate-controlled aquarium, only to be released into the wild when it became so large it could no longer be handled safely, by an owner who didn't have the heart to kill it. Regardless, the deed done here today by the creature was not for justice, nor for revenge, rather, it was done by a creature who acted purely upon instinct, fighting for its own survival. In satisfying its appetite, it became the executioner that administered the required death sentence.

Unwilling to relent, the monstrous serpent continued to hold its prey for a half hour or so after all movement had ceased. Uncoiling... the massive snake made its way towards Rico's head. Unhinging its jaw, it proceeded to...

Chapter Twenty-Four: Come Fly with Me

"You know Beth, I've been thinking about all this. About Ohio Jim, the clues in the letter, his death and everything else that has come down the pike lately. When Ohio Jim said he lied about where he found the coin, you know? It got me to thinking. I think Ohio Jim found the whole dam thing."

"The whole thing?"

"Yes Beth, I think he found the whole treasure. I think the clues in the letter tell exactly where it is too if we can just figure them out."

"We found the coin in his house exactly where he said it was. Covered in flour, in the plate of sand dollars. Remember? "What we held is with the dollars in my house" that was Fairly clever, I'd say. Let's give this all some thought and see what we can come up with. Try to organize it to get some meaning out of it."

"Sure Curt, I'm not really sure what you're saying but I'll follow your lead."

"Thanks Hun. Hey, it's 11:15 and I am starving! Want some lunch?

How bout the City Yacht Club, does that sound good to you?"

"Sure, let's go for it." Beth piped in.

"You know, I love the Cape. The four lane streets everywhere makes it effortless to navigate the city." Curt headed south down Coronado Boulevard towards the restaurant. With ease his Jeep found its way to the club where he glided into a parking space, right in front of the Yacht Club Tiki Bar. "Looks like we made it just in time before the rush."

Smiling, Curt reached across the center console and patted Beth's knee. "You ready dear?"

"I think so, it's all been so crazy lately, I can hardly remember when I last ate something that was really good and filling."

"Well, the food here is really good and there is such a great view of the Caloosahatchee River, I thought it would give us some time together to relax and think about everything that's happened lately. They have great hamburgers and incredible peel and eat shrimp too."

"After we eat, like I said, perhaps we can organize Ohio Jim's clues and talk through the recent events and see it we come up with anything."

"Ok, Sounds good."

Curt and Beth walked up the stairs towards the nonsmoking food deck.

"Let's sit over there so we can see the water and the pier too."

"This is almost strange that we are here. Like fate has aligned to call me back, you know. I mean this isn't someplace where we usually go."

"Curt, right up there at the bar is where I first met Ohio Jim, can you believe it? Looks like an innocent conversation, while having a cold beer, started this whole thing."

"Oh, wow Beth, I think you told me that. Guess I forgot about it."

Curt picked up the menu and looked at it while Beth checked her phone.

"I think I'm going to have a big Shrimp cocktail and a burger. What sounds good to you?"

"I'll try the burger too Curt. But I think the Cole slaw, sounds a lot better than fries. I don't think I can stand the grease."

"Sure Hon, I understand, gotcha."

As Curt glanced up, away from the menu, from around the far corner of the bar, a friend of Curt's suddenly appeared.

Curt stood up and called to him. PJ. Curt waved.

When Curt first moved to Cape Coral, early one Saturday morning, he found himself going to some garage sales searching

171

for some bargains on a few utilitarian items for his new home. That's where he first met PJ. Since then, Curt always calls PJ his oldest friend in the Cape and they still manage to run across each other from time to time.

"Dude, how you been?"

"Good. Good Curt, how've you been?"

"Absolutely great. Hey, let me introduce you to my girlfriend. PJ, this is Beth, Beth Higgins."

"Nice to meet you PJ."

"Likewise, Mam."

"Paul Johnson is his real name. We call him PJ for short."

"PJ, have you been fishing lately?"

"Every day Curt. Season is in full swing now. I've been having at least one charter every day for quite a while."

"Anything fun biting?"

"Well; Pompano, Speckled Sea Trout, Mackerel and Gag Grouper have been hitting pretty good.

Why, You two want to go catch some fish?"

"Well, no, I just wondered how business was. We've got a lot on our plate right now but, I promise, we will give you a call as soon as we can get some free time."

"Sounds Good," PJ said.

"PJ, aren't you a Florida's son so to speak? A Florida Cracker?"

"Yup, Born and raised here."

"So, you grew up fishing this entire area and these waters, right?

Yes, ever since I was a pup, that's all I can remember, fishing with my Grandpa and my Dad. From the head waters of the Caloosahatchee river near Arcadia up north, south, thru all the islands clear to Boca Grande Pass and Charlotte Harbor."

"So, what are you now, about 35 years old or so?"

"Pretty close." PJ said proudly.

"That's a lot of fishing. I'll bet you've covered about every inch of every estuary in this entire fishery, haven't you?"

"Well, I'd sure like to think so." PJ said humbly.

"PJ, come to think of it, I'd like to ask you a question. Does the word Darling mean anything to you?"

"Darling? No, not really. You mean like a little darling. Ha, just kidding! No, wait, now that I think about it, there's a tiny mangrove key up north in the Pine Island Sound area called Darling Key."

"Seriously, Curt said squinting his brow, with an expression of surprise on his face. Curt turned to look at Beth then back at PJ. Seriously?" He uttered again. "There's a small mangrove key called Darling key?"

"Curt, it's absolutely tiny, no good for anything. It's just a spot on the map. It's on the western channel edge just about a mile north of Wilson Cut when you leave Pineland Marina."

"Oh, Ok, No biggy. I just wondered." Curt said." Someone had mentioned the name and I just wondered if it were a real place."

"Yup, It's real alright. Too small for shit, but it's real. Oh, excuse my language Mam."

Beth smiled and nodded.

"Well, there you have it. Great to see you but, Look Curt, I've got to run, I still have to get my rods ready for tomorrows trip and I have to go by the bait shop and pick up some hooks I ordered. Hope you both have a nice lunch. It was my pleasure meeting you Mam."

"Thank You, PJ, that's very sweet of you."

"See you guys."

"Best of Luck to you PJ. Catch lots of fish and we'll call you as soon as we get loose."

"Have a nice lunch. See Ya."

PJ exited the bar area and took off in the direction of the parking lot where his truck was parked.

Curt turned to Beth. "Oh My God Beth. Did you hear that. A tiny mangrove key called Darling Key?"

"If I'm not mistaken Ohio Jim said: "A tiny Key Will unlock the treasure" and "I miss my DARLING Jennis". Something tells me that the mystery has just been taken out of this whole thing girl. Let's go ahead and order lunch. Once we've finished eating, I think it would be cool if we took a trip up in the Pine Island sound area and took a look around."

"Whatever you think is fine with me Curt."

"I can rent a Jet Ranger Helicopter by the hour at Paige field off highway 41 in Ft Myers. It'll just be a hop and a skip up there that way. Have you ever been in a helicopter?"

"No, I can't say as I have. Is it safe?" Beth said looking over towards Curt's cane.

Picking up on Beth's insinuation, Curt confidently said; "Sure, as long as no one is shooting at us." Besides, I've seen it, it's a fine machine. It's almost brand new. I can fly it as well, if not better than I drive my own car too. My License is still in full force."

"Ok, I'm game. I'll give it a try."

"This way Beth, we can get a bird's eye view of the little Darling key without having to wait. Truthfully, after getting this news, I don't think I could sleep a wink tonight If I had to wait until tomorrow before we could go up there."

"Sure then, Why not? Let's give it a go."

Curt practically inhaled his lunch.

With both hands atop his cane for balance, from his toe up to his knee, Curt's leg bounced nervously up and down as he waited for Beth to finish her lunch.

"Waiter. Excuse me. Will you bring me the check please?"

"Certainly Sir. Another glass of tea for you Mam?"

"No Thank You. I'm good."

Curt paid cash, so he wouldn't have to wait around for the credit card voucher to come back for his signature.

Normally, Curt was calm and very easy going but at this moment, he was wound up tighter than a banjo string.

"Ready to go dear?"

"Yes, Curt. Honestly right now I can't tell if your excitement comes from the possibility of finding a multi-million-dollar Spanish treasure or if it's the opportunity for you to get to fly your precious Jet Ranger helicopter. Whatever, either way, it sounds exotic and exciting. I'm in. Let's go."

Curt and Beth left the restaurant, piled into the Jeep and headed back towards mainstream Cape Coral.

Once on the Boulevard, Curt pointed. "Look, there's a West Marine store. I'm going to take a moment and make a quick stop in there."

Curt wheeled the Jeep into the parking lot. "I think I'll run in and see if they have some sort of geographical or nautical map that would show the local landmarks."

"Sure, great idea Beth replied, go ahead, I'll stay here with the car."

Curt went inside and was back in a flash. Once in the car, opening the seal on the package, Curt unfolded the map and stared at it.

"Look at this Beth. Curt pointed, look right there. What's that say? Darling Key?"

"Yes, it certainly does."

As they headed over the Big Cape Coral bridge, Curt called ahead to Paige field and made the arrangements for the use of the Jet Ranger.

"You know, Curt, ever since I met you my life seems to have stepped up in pace. I used to be just a lowly archeologist who occasionally got her hands dirty."

"You! Oh my God! From the day I met you it's been almost insane. First a man dies. Then we go on a wild goose chase for treasure, then there's a kidnapping that results in a mass gang shooting, obviously it seems, I may have bit off more than I can chew and what's worse, I may be starting to enjoy it all, dammit!"

Both Curt and Beth broke into laughter. Beth's smile was magnetic to Curt. He found it hard to keep his eyes on the road for wanting to look at her. As Curt continued towards Paige field, Beth gazed out of the window at the water below the bridge. How beautiful it all was. What a great day to still be alive.

Turning off highway 41, Curt headed the Jeep over to the parking and receiving area of the Sea Star Flight Service. Curt stopped, shut the motor off, depressed the button and shoved the shift handle forward into Park.

"Just give me just a minute. I'll run in and finish the rental agreement dear."

It wasn't long, and Curt walked back to the car with a packet of papers in his hand. "Beth, will you put these in the glove box for me please."

Sure.

Curt opened the car door for Beth. They walked across the tarmac to where the helicopter was being fueled.

Once the fuel truck moved, Curt walked around the craft to begin his pre-flight check.

"Look's good. What a beauty you are, turning to Beth." he said with a big grin." BOTH OF YOU."

"Oh, stop it and do what you have to do Silly boy."

Curt blushed, then turned to finish his pre-flight.

Curt crawled in, secured his cane, then turned to help Beth.

"Ok, hop on in here dear, fasten your seatbelt and put these headphones on. Then we'll get started."

"Let's see. Battery switch engage full. Master fuel valve on, zero all gauges, check all fuses overhead, all good."

"OK, Check stall warning alarm, Good." Curt popped open the small side window and yelled: "CLEAR All CLEAR."

"Let's see, left hand, twists the throttle to reset, then left now and back to the right, push the red button in and turn it back for low fuel input. "

"CLEAR!" Curt yelled out again.

"Now with the right–hand index finger hit the starter button. Engage the turbine, now twist the left hand to give it some fuel slightly. Let the turbine start the wind up towards grand idle. We'll get the power turbine and rotor speed up to 100 % in just a second. Then it's all is good."

"Now let's check the angle of the main blade and tail rotor. Full power up to 100%."

"READY to go dear? All we do is lift the bar, center up and back on the stick, up we go."

Curt lifted the helicopter up and hovered over the pad. Then called the tower.

"Helicopter Echo Bravo Tango Ranger to tower, permission to take off from Sea Star Aviation please?"

"Roger Helicopter Echo Bravo Tango Ranger, permission granted, squawk 357niner on your transponder, exit left from the pad on a 185–degree heading, winds South SW at 6 mph, altimeter 0004, contact departure when you are out of the pattern. Good day Sir."

"Roger, 357niner, 185 degrees departure. Thank You Sir, Good Day."

Curt gently coaxed the Bell 206 Ranger upward into the sky, headed west then turned south towards Sanibel on the prescribed heading.

"This is nice, Beth said, thru the headset, a bit loud but it's cool."

"It's awesome. I was beginning to miss flying more and more each day. Beth, honey, will you spread that map out, so I can see the area up north around pine island. Yes, that's great dear. Thank You. We're VFR today."

Beth looked puzzled.

Curt turned, "Visual Flight Rules today," Curt said. "Not being familiar with the area from above, I've decided to take the route that would allow us to keep the islands in sight for navigational purposes. I've been up that way by car before. This route will put us over Sanibel just on the other side of Blind pass then, we'll go on up north over Captiva island. Looks like somewhere about right there, near Redfish pass, we should angle to the northeast towards the Pineland Marina area, then we'll head north again from Wilson Cut."

Beth looked over at Curt admiringly and smiled.

The time passed quickly as they cut through the air towards their destination.

"It's all so beautiful from up here." Beth said. "Look you can see both sides of the islands and the water color is breathtaking. I'm so glad we are doing this. I've been on these islands hundreds of times but not until today did I know area was this beautiful and magnificent. The boats look so tiny."

"Speaking of tiny Beth. Look right over there! See that little spec of an island?" Curt pointed.

"Yes, I see it."

"Well, just like Ohio Jim said; judging from the spot on the map, that's the tiny key that may unlock the treasure. It's Darling Key."

"It looks kind of like the island is split doesn't it?"

"Maybe it's just a split in the mangrove overgrowth. I don't know, let's take it a little lower and get a better look."

Curt rotated the craft holding it to a tight circle above the little key to get a better view while allowing himself to decrease his altitude.

"Curt, Look! What's that big brown thing over there? It looks like a big tree trunk or a log or something. What do you think?"

"I don't know what that it is Beth, but there's some rock exposed right there at the top of that part of the key on the right. I'm going to take us just a touch lower?"

"I agree, it looks like there's a series of old weathered conch shells lined up at the apex of that little limestone ridge.

That's funny girl, for a moment I forgot that I was with a world renown Archeologist. Good observation Beth."

"Oh, stop it. Can you see what I'm talking about? That has to be manmade."

"Yes, I can Beth. I think it's worth a closer look, don't you?"

"Not in this bird though."

"We can't land the helicopter here can we?"

"No, but we've seen enough to know that this is definitely what we came for. What do you say? It's getting late in the afternoon. Let's get the chopper back and make some plans for a boat rental tomorrow and come back then."

"Sounds good to me." Beth said.

"Curt rotated the helicopter around in a big sweeping circle, gained some altitude and headed back towards the field.

With the flip of an auxiliary switch to WAVE 101.1, Curt managed to fill their headphones with the easy listening music of Sade.

179

Looking down, out through the clear Plex canopy flooring of the helicopter, Beth sighed. "It's an incredibly stunning view from up here."

Curt smiled at her, then turned to re-focus his attention out front.

Upon arriving back at Sea Star Aviation, "That was fabulous." Beth exclaimed; as she exited the helicopter. "I never realized how much fun that could be."

"I have always loved it." Curt said. "It's feels like such freedom and convenience at the same time."

"I'm just looking ahead a touch, doing some mental planning so, would you like to stay at my house tonight dear or do you have other plans?"

"If you are a cookin, then I'm a stayin." Beth said. Lovingly, she mocked his southern draw in fun.

"Beth honestly, I don't know what I'm going to do with you."

"Well... you could start by taking me to your house and fixing me a cocktail. She said with a mischievous smile. It's warm tonight and swim might be nice."

Beth always uses a sensual provocative approach to life which usually results in her getting her way. At any given moment, she may tilt her head and raise an eyebrow as if to pose a question which, usually catches Curt off guard or hits him in his soft spot. It's amazing just how easily he stumbles into the trap she sets. Eager to complete her desires, he falls right in. Her radiant green eyes combined with an infectious smile is hard to say no too. On numerous occasions Curt has admitted that, just the sight of her alone leaves him in awe.

"You Got it." Curt said, as he fired up the Jeep. "Boogie Board Cocktails and a moonlight swim coming up." Curt put the truck in gear but didn't move. Reaching over, he placed his hand on her knee, raised his eyes to meet hers and smiled. "Did you always get your way as a child Beth?"

"I did! Most of the time she pronounced emphatically. Most always, come to think of it."

"Then It shall be done. As You Wish my dear."

Curt took his foot off the brake and rolled on out to the traffic light where he made a brief stop, then turned right out onto 41 heading back on Boy Scout Drive towards his house.

As Curt drove on, Beth stared at the hair on his forearms and his strong hands, the way his fingers wrapped around the steering wheel. She glanced up at his unshaven jaw line then, returned her gaze to the windshield.

For having such strength, at times, he demonstrated an incredibly soft touch she thought. Starring ahead, she smiled. Perhaps, it was the overload of the aerial visual stimulation of day. Maybe it was the vibrations of the Helicopter ride that filled Beth's senses to the brim. Regardless of what it was that raised her level of excitement, there seemed to be something in the air indicating that this night would end up with a very happy ending.

Chapter Twenty-Five: A Tiny Key Unlocks the Treasure

"Why so early?"

"I've got a lot to do each morning to make myself presentable."
Beth bounded out of bed and headed for the kitchen.

Covering his head partially with his pillow to shield his eyes, he
spoke through the pillowcase. "You are the best-looking
morning riser I've ever seen. So, I don't buy it."

"Well, that's very sweet of you Curt but, this hair and makeup
won't do themselves. I have to coax it into place every morning,
so I need a little extra time to get it all done, besides, I like to
leisurely sip my home coffee brew to get each day headed in the
right direction."

"Ok, I got you on that but, why would you want to get up so
early when you don't have to go to your office?"

Curt had been retired from the service for several years, so he
didn't really care what time he woke up each morning. Unless,
of course he had an early appointment to get his car serviced or
something like that.

Beth, on the other hand, was always up at 5:30 every morning.

"Oh My! "Mr. I'm excited to go flying man." I guess I'm excited
to go to the dig. Remember? I can't believe you are acting so lazy
after all we discovered yesterday."

"Oh Yah, I remember, we found an island that's been there since
the beginning of time and we have to get up at the crack of dawn
and rush right back to make sure it's still there."

"CURT!"

"I'm just kidding you Beth. I guess it was the cocktails and the
swim last night that wore me out."

With a big smile, Beth eyes met Curt's.

"Get up you lazy bones. Don't make me come get you out of that
bed."

"Woo are you threatening me."

"Maybe!"

"That could be fun." Curt said.

"Look, it's tempting, and it sounds wonderful, but we need to get going."

"Oh, alright." Curt slide sideways out of the covers on the bed, stood up and shuffled his way off to the bathroom.

"You want some coffee Sweetie?"

"Does a wild man eat berries in the forest? Sure, I'd love some."

"Ok dear, one black Café Verona coffee coming up."

Beth made her way back to the pot on the kitchen service island and poured some coffee into Curt's favorite cup. Returning to the bathroom, she sat his cup down on the cabinet next to his toothbrush holder.

"Thank You so much you Little Darling. Well, there ya have it, I made another funny."

With a big grin on his face, Curt wiped the toothpaste off his chin, then picked up his cup and took a sip of the coffee. "Umm Boy, that's some good stuff right there. I love that Gold Coast roast."

"It's not Gold Coast dear. I switched it on you. Doesn't it taste a little bit Smokey to you? It's Starbucks Café Verona espresso ground."

"You are so tricky and yes, it's marvelous dear. Let me take a quick rinse in the shower and I'll be right out."

"Sure, go for it. I'm going to answer some texts from school. Do we need to call the marina about the boat?"

"Nope, I took care of that last night. All we have to do is show up, get checked out and away we go. It's going to be fun. From the map, Darling key is only ten minutes away at the most, so it won't take us long to get there, once we get started."

"OK, I'll be ready when you are."

"Curt, when you get dressed, be sure to wear your water shoes. It's been my experience that those mangrove keys are always covered with extremely sharp-edged oyster shells. Mine are in my car, I'll get them. We sure don't need to suffer an un-necessary injury today. Lots of bacteria in those shells too. You just never know."

Ok. Will do. Good thinking Beth. My Protectorate hath Spoken! Silly Boy.

"We'll it makes good sense. Glad you thought of it. Anything else?"

"Absolutely, Bug spray. The number one thing you never leave the house without if you are near a mangrove key is bug spray. I'm telling you, without it, any number of bugs will eat us alive."

"Wow, I would never have thought of that."

"See, I really am handy to have around."

"You certainly are dear. I hate bug bites and I don't know if I ever said anything about it but I'm allergic to some bugs bites, wasps for sure."

"I doubt there will be any wasps, but you never know. One thing is for sure, they'll be plenty of Mosquitos and No-see-ums that are vicious biting machines out there."

"Dude! I hate Skeetos."

"Here, spray this on your legs and put some of this cream on your arms and face."

"Thank You dear. I feel safer already."

Curt and Beth loaded up in the Jeep and made their way over to Pine Island then turned on Stringfellow Rd. and headed North on towards their destination.

"I rented a 24' center console."

"Center console?" Beth questioned.

"Yes, the steering wheel and controls are on a pedestal located in the center of the boat. It lets you walk completely around the gunnels inside of the boat. Actually, the design effectively, makes the boat larger for use. I made sure there was a ladder on the stern too. In case we need it."

"Good thinking. Ok, sounds good to me. This will be fun! Is that it over there? Oh! What a nice marina."

Along the road a large red and black arrow pointing westward indicated they had arrived. Left turn to Four Winds Marina. Curt carefully brought the Jeep to a stop in the parking area.

"Beth, see over there, Curt pointed, that's the boat we'll be using alongside the dock. How about you take our stuff over to it and I'll go in and take care of the rental."

"Sure, I'll do it."

Curt helped Beth gather the things they would need for the days outing, then she turned and made her way towards the boat. Curt watched her walk away towards the rental. With each stride, he saw the muscles in her long tan legs flex as she gracefully made her way along the path. "What a beautiful creature," he said to himself.

After the boat checkout, Curt and Beth made their way out of the marina harbor, down the canal towards Pine Island Sound. Once they cleared the manatee slow zone, Curt raised the throttle and brought the boat up on plane, steering it between the channel markers then turning to the west. A half mile out, glancing down at the GPS viewer screen, Curt looked up, raised his hand and pointed.

"That's it over there Beth."

"I'm so excited. This could be the greatest discovery of my career." Beth exclaimed.

As they approached, Curt slowed the boat down and smiled. He maneuvered through the shallow waters towards the east side of the little island.

"I guess we'll see if Ohio Jim was right. Today we find out if indeed, if a Tiny Key will unlock the treasure."

As they approached, the water depth lessened to only a foot deep or so. "We'll probably have to wade in then crawl up to where you saw the limestone crest yesterday and that row of old shells."

Curt continued to pull back on the throttle and raised the motor on the boat to its highest position as the boat ceased its forward motion.

Over the side of the gunnel he lifted his leg and eased down into the water.

"It's shallow here, don't worry he told Beth."

She looked at him trustfully and acknowledged.

Grabbing the bow line, he took a few steps and tied the boat off to a mangrove limb.

Coming back to the boat he extended his arms.

"Here Hon, let me help you down."

As Beth made her way dangling her legs over the side. Curt reached up to brace her, placing his hands steadily under her armpits. Gently he allowed her to slide slowly down out of the boat, completely into his grip.

Without realizing it, Curt was holding her full weight in his hands about 2 inches off the bottom of the sandy key flat.

Again, they found themselves so close. Face to face the sunlight accentuated the beautiful colors in their reflective eyes as they fixated upon each other.

Instantly, huge feelings welled up from deep down inside him. Pushing their way up, up like a missile launching from inside. What's happening he thought. Were these the same feelings of

186

helplessness he felt the night that Beth was kidnapped? Were these the feelings that came from deep down inside that he felt when he realized he loved her, when he felt he might lose her forever. Feelings he could do nothing about.

NO, not at all, this was completely different. Though, again Beth was the reason, these were feelings of a different sort. Feelings he knew he could do something about. Exhilaration, Joy and Celebration could be the only words to describe his elation.

Like an explosion, his deep voice rattled with excitement:

"Beth! I Love You! You are so beautiful and just, so you know, before we go off and find some multi-million-dollar treasure, while we're still poor, I want you to know that... I Love You Beth. I love you with all my heart."

Instantly, Beth burst into tears of joy that streamed down her face.

"Curt, Oh My God...Curt, I love You so much. You will never know how much I love you. I don't know why I have been so blessed, but I am willing to take this wherever it leads us. This is the greatest day of my life. Regardless of what happens, today I have truly found the greatest treasure of all."

Beth wrapped both her arms around his neck. Feverishly they kissed one another. She kissed him as though each kiss could never end, nor would it ever be enough to satisfy her desire for him.

Almost having to pull away from her, Curt mustered a breath.

"Dam it girl, this is a hell of a place for this to happen. But I have to admit, I've never been so happy about anything in my life.

If only Ohio Jim could have known that this Tiny Key would unlock the treasure our love. I know he would have been proud."

Curt gently lowered her until her feet could touch the key flat bottom, then he reached back into the boat to grab a towel.

"Here, let me wipe your face dear."

Beth smiled as they shared opposite ends of the towel to wipe the sweat and tears from their faces. Regaining their composure, Curt offered his hand to her, as they left the boat and waded ahead towards the dry area of the key.

"Watch that oyster bed. You are right, those shell edges are sharp."

"I told you."

"I know you did dear and you were right. Bugs, tons of bugs. I hate them. Hell, I can't even breath without getting them in my mouth. Every time, they get me. It's like they lie in wait, watching for me to come along, then they attack."

"I know, I've had to put up with them for years on the digs I've been on here in Florida."

Beth and Curt carefully made their way and shimmied up the sloped side of the tiny limestone outcrop.

"Look, this seems to be a roof like area that's been closed off. See, the shells you saw yesterday are definitely part of it. They're encased in some sort of ancient mortar or plaster of some kind.

"Mind if I take a look Curt?"

"Oh, Sorry Hon. Be my guest Dr. Higgins, please do."

Curt gestured to her extending his hand to give her support. "Up you go!"

Once atop the structure, Beth turned to look back at Curt. Instantly, her mouth dropped open as she stared over his shoulder, then screamed.

"Curt, IT'S ALIVE."

Curt spun around to see a heavily incumbered serpent form lift its head looking back in his direction.

"Unreal! That's what we saw from the helicopter yesterday, that thing that I thought looked like a tree trunk or log. Curt, it's a monster snake, I kid you not."

"I see it Beth. Calm down now hon."

Curt sized up the situation, regained his composure and spoke; "It's obviously killed something huge and swallowed it. That's for sure. It's so heavily laden, I don't think it can even move. I'll bet that thing is 30 feet long or better. I know that the authorities are trying to eliminate those big snakes from the Florida wild. All of them are invasive species. I'm not familiar with the big constrictor snakes but this one, whatever it is, most likely, it will prove to be amongst the largest on earth. The first thing we need to do after we leave here is notify the Florida Wildlife Commission about it."

"I agree Curt. They will probably send someone out here to kill it. I think they should cut it open and see what's inside it. Look at its eyes Curt, they seem to follow us."

"Wow, you're right Beth, they do."

"What do you think it swallowed?"

"I'd say a key deer or a wild hog or something like that."

"From the looks of it, that would be some big wild hog. Do you think it will try to bother us?"

"Like I said Beth, I don't think that thing will even be able to move for at least a week or two."

"I hope you are right; I don't want that ugly thing coming after us."

"Whoa! Me neither."

"I think we'll be alright. Besides, we're going that way." Curt pointed.

"Ok, I trust your judgment." Beth turned her attention back to the outcrop. As she edged near the row of shells at the apex of the dome, she noticed an opening in the mortar. Possibly erosion due to extended weathering she thought.

"LOOK! Look here Curt, there's a little hole in the covering. I can see inside. I...UNBELIEVABLE! I see GOLD. Gold Curt. Lots of gold. We've found it! I see some coins in there too, like the one Jim found." Beth carefully reached inside and pulled a coin out for better viewing. "I can see some gold bars and lots of other lose artifacts too."

"The Legend of the Pass is no longer a mystery. It's now officially true." Beth announced.

Carefully, she knelt down to look closer into the hole. With the small hammer she carried in her belt, she chipped away a little bit more of the mortar to get a better look.

"Curt, this is incredible, it looks like a number of rotted chests, stacked on top of each other, more loose coins and artifacts. Lots and lots of stuff in there. Jim was right. A Tiny key did Unlock the Treasure."

"Amongst other things." Curt said, as he grinned gleefully.

"Indeed." she said with a big smile.

"Judging from the lateral extent that this roof covers, opposed by the width, if it's all full of treasure, then there's going to be a bunch of it."

"Perhaps an entire ship load." Curt answered.

"Absolutely. I think we should leave now before we attract any attention. We'll get the school behind this at once, least we lose it to the State authorities on some technicality treasure finding law or something."

"Good thinking Beth. Let's leave it like we found it, go back, and get the school stamp on the excavation to validate it all. Then make the claim."

"Sounds like a plan. Let's get to it. Hey, before we go, how bout we put this dead mangrove branch over the hole, so no one will see it. Better yet, if I stick this end in the hole, it will look like it grew out of the rock. That way, no one will get any ideas."

"Ok, sounds good."

They were very careful with every step they took descending from the outcrop. As they approached, the giant snake raised it head once again.

"Those eyes give me the creeps Curt."

"No kidding. Sinister, aren't they?"

"Yes, and it's a good thing that monster has already eaten. Dam let's get out of here."

They exercised extreme caution as they eased past the area where the snake lay incapacitated. Beth and Curt entered the water and waded back to the boat. Curt extended the ladder then offered Beth his hand.

Once back inside, Beth looked back towards the little island, then she turned to look at Curt.

"You know something Dear; I can truly say that today, I have officially found the Two Greatest Treasures of my life."

Curt smiled and agreed.

Chapter Twenty-Six: What's Up Dr. Higgins?

Of late, Curt and Beth have been making a habit of meeting up together at Starbucks each morning before she had to leave for her office. The line was short this morning so getting their coffee went much faster than usual.

"Glad to see the place a little less crowded. Sometimes it's like pulling teeth just to get a Latte around here."

"Let's set here Beth. You know, It's funny. Each time we come here I think of the first time we met. This is where it all began, remember?" Curt smiled as he cleared a place on the table.

"Yes, I do." she said.

Beth Looked in his direction, then down to the table where she saw a copy of the local Cape Coral Breeze newspaper.

Front Page headlines read; Florida Wildlife Commission autopsies captured, giant invasive snake. A partially decomposed body of prominent Miami businessman found inside.

"Beth picked up the paper and said. Oh My God. Look, the Miami businessman was identified as Enrique Ribeiro. Curt, I swear that's the guy that came in and questioned me when I was kidnapped."

"What makes you say that Beth?"

"Cause one of the kidnappers screwed up and called him Rico. That's short for Enrique. He ate the guys ass out for calling him by name too."

Well, that explains the little boat they found covered up with those mangrove branches. He probably used it to make it over to the little key. Curt reasoned.

"I wonder how he ended up at Darling key anyway." Beth asked.

"I Guess he figured it out from the clues just like we did."

Beth pointed at the paper again.

"Yes, most likely with Alvera's help. How else would he have known about the coin or the treasure in order to end up at Darling Key? "

"Well, I'm dam glad he did too, or it could have been one of us that big snake latched on to. Dam! What a way to go."

"You have to admit, that was an eerie, disturbing sight, seeing that giant snake incapacitated so close to where we found the treasure."

"If the truth be known, it was probably Dr. Alvera that was in cahoots with this guy from the beginning after overhearing your conversation with Ohio Jim. He probably put him onto the whole dam thing. Think about it. Beth. Dr. Alvera was also, most likely killed by this guy."

"Hell, there's been a line of dead bodies since this whole thing started. You know it's funny too, they couldn't assign a 100% cause of death from the autopsy on Alvera. It's just all way too coincidental for me."

"That's right Curt. It's actually so obvious now. You know, I still feel bad about Ohio Jim though. He was just a sweet, simple man with a big secret."

"Yeah and if he hadn't shared it with you Beth, everything would be a whole lot different than it is right now."

"Yes, but I think that fate always seeks to fulfill itself regardless of who tries to interfere."

"Perhaps you're right."

"Did I show you the list of all the artifacts that were recovered from Darling Key? After the entire cavity was excavated and all the contents removed, here's what they found inside:"

"600 bars of pure gold along with many gold-inlaid and gold covered artifacts. Also, there were 30 Chests of gold coins.
600 bars of gold $43,464.900 at $1293.60 per oz.
Gold and gold overlaid ancient artifacts $21,000,000.
$64,464,960.00
The 30 chest of gold coins contained 2000 coins per chest equals 4.5 billion each coin averaging $75,000 each."
"Let's see, three, carry the one, that's a bunch." Curt smiled.

"Well, the college went from a small center of learning to a financial powerhouse in demand overnight."
"I know that 4 billion dollars made a big difference on their bottom line."
"You should see the plans the President and Deans are making. Not to mention I was told that you and I would be receiving a check for a nice round figure of, I think it was; five million dollars apiece, taxes paid."

"Are you serious?" Curt looked up. "Unbelievable. It's like we both just won the Florida Lottery at the same time."
"Now, I'm going to be hard to live with, I just know it. Beth. Just kidding. Other than the possibility that a new boat now looms in my future, I doubt my life will change much. Oh, I may pay off my house too come to think of it. That is so very generous of them."
"Sounds like some intelligent moves to me on your part, paying off your house and such."
"There ya go, getting all that formal, responsible stuff going again."
"Well, when you think about it, if we hadn't found it, the school wouldn't have had any claim to the treasure."

"Yes, and I think it was a clever idea having the school cover the discovery like it was one of their many science and excavation digs. Good move on your part Beth, otherwise the State of Florida may have moved in and took it all over."

"Exactly, I don't trust those State and Federal boys when money and treasure is involved. Remember what happened to Mel Fisher. Mel looked for years and spent countless thousands, then when he discovered the Atocha, it was almost taken away from him."

"I know all about it Beth. Remember the book I was carrying the day we met?"

"I do remember Curt."

"So, when do you get to start handing out all those scholarships and grants?" "Once you start doing that, you'll most likely put this little college on the list of the most desirable schools in the nation."

After all, You're now the Dr. with the nationally known licensed Arch shovel. They will storm you no doubt."

"Perhaps it will. I'm going to try to do all the grant evaluations myself for a while. At least until the demand takes more time than I can give. Then, I guess we'll have to hire additional faculty to process all the apps."

"Good problems I'd say. Just think, you have the gift of learning for many a deserving student available at the mere stroke of your pen."

Beth smiled, "Yes, I agree, these are all good problems. I'm not only grateful, I'm looking forward to it."

"I know you are dear. I know your heart. It's an awesome opportunity as well as a great responsibility."

"Did I tell you; they're naming the new museum after us? The Higgins Lafferty Cultural Center and Museum. It has a nice ring to it, don't you think?"

"I do." Curt answered.

"Uncovering the Past, Seeking Today's Knowledge"

"Pretty good slogan too. You know where that came from don't you?"

"I don't, Beth, but I have a feeling you're a fixin to tell me."

"Well, all the students at FSW were asked to make up and submit a slogan. The one that was chosen would be placed up front top, under the building name, carved in marble and that was the one that was selected."

"That's pretty Cool, Curt said. Get the whole school involved and make them a part of the discovery while doing it."

"So that goes under the name of the building out front eh?"

"Yes, it does. Inside the building, they will display some of what we found and part of the limestone remnant that held the treasure for those many years, for all to see. They want to excavate a portion of the key to recreate the scene of how it was actually found."

"Cool Beth, you better not forget to honor Ohio Jim with a presentation on him too. Perhaps, tell his story and all about the clues he left. You know dear, to this day I can't look at a pair of those white, rubber fishermen's boots, that I don't think of him."

"Interesting Curt. Yes, that's the least we can do. I'll give that some serious thought."

Sounds creative. So, Beth, now that you are a famous International Archeologist what are your plans? Do you think you will take Dr. Fuentes up on his invitation to visit Colombia? I saw the letter from him you left on the service counter at my house. You know, he's hoping you'll help him find the Lost City of Emeralds in the Colombian Andes, don't you?"

"Truthfully, Curt, there's been so much going on, I haven't had time to think about it. I Guess "Every Trip is an Adventure" from here on out."

"I guess it is dear."

"Beth, Honey. I have some errands to take care of this morning and I need to run by Galeana Jeep to check on the spare tire cover I ordered. You'll be headed into your office before too long, won't you?"

"I will indeed Mr. Jonathan Curtis Lafferty."

Laughing out loud Curt said, "Beth dear, I know it's early to be talking about this and we're only, just now having our morning coffee, but I'd like to ask you before I go. Do you have any plans for tonight? "

"No, not really, none that I can think of."

"Well, I was thinking. What I'd really like tonight, is a big tender filet cut from Publix, baked tater and a nice chilled glass of Merlot out by the pool."

"So, Beth; would you like to join me for dinner tonight?"

"Absolutely Curt! I'd love too."

The End

About the Author

Captain Russell D Walker is a Professional Fishing

Guide in South West Florida

Author

Poet

&

Local and Marine Artist

Pen name Muddoggie

Lives in Cape Coral, Fl. With his wife Julia

198

Made in USA - Kendallville, IN
1219807_9781983114922